P9-DWC-037

TWO AGAINST A LYNCH MOB

The rising shout of anger was suddenly stilled as the leaders stared into the black muzzle of a Winchester .44/40 carbine.

Ki spoke now, and made no speech out of it: "Break it up! Or I will!"

For an instant there was stunned silence. It was shattered by the craggy-browed man's howl of wrath. "Who in hell are you to barge up here and tell folks what to do?"

Instantly the carbine muzzle moved a trifle, until it was lined on the craggy man's broad chest. "This's me. You want an introduction?"

The color drained from the craggy man's face and he seemed to shrivel as he slipped aside from under Ki's point-blank range.

Then there was a clatter of hoofs, and Jessie rode to the front, her rented horse plowing another shock wave of tumbling men through the mob. Dismounting at a run, she joined Ki, her carbine grasped firmly...

WESLEY ELLIS

LONE STAR

AND THE
¡PHANTOM GUNMEN

JOVE BOOKS, NEW YORK

LONE STAR AND THE PHANTOM GUNMEN

A Jove Book / published by arrangement with
the author

PRINTING HISTORY
Jove edition / November 1987

All rights reserved.
Copyright © 1987 by Jove Publications, Inc.
This book may not be reproduced in whole or in part,
by mimeograph or any other means, without permission.
For information address: The Berkley Publishing Group,
200 Madison Avenue, New York, New York 10016.

ISBN: 0-515-09257-6

Jove Books are published by The Berkley Publishing Group,
200 Madison Avenue, New York, New York 10016.
The name "JOVE" and the "J" logo
are trademarks belonging to Jove Publications, Inc.

PRINTED IN THE UNITED STATES OF AMERICA

10 9 8 7 6 5 4 3 2 1

Chapter 1

"Watch out!" Ki yelled.

Too late. His sharp, startled warning was cut by a thunderous explosion. The railroad trestle dead ahead burst into flashfire and powder smoke, and a shock wave jolted the tracks beneath their onrushing train. Flung off balance, Jessica Starbuck jounced skidding from her seat as the coach shook violently, rattling and quaking. Ki, leaning out the window, held tight to the sill, staring, alarmed at the eruption that was sundering the trestle and sending wreckage cascading down into the deep, wide arroyo below. The log framework swayed, then listed, its deck planks crumbling and steel rails buckling. Adjacent chunks of span fell loose, widening the gaping hole.

The aged bell-stack locomotive plunged for the hole, taking the string of five old cars with it.

The coach lurched and tilted, dumping Jessie and another woman passenger in a tangled sprawl. Ki pitched back, stumbling away from the window, scarcely able to grab Jessie by one arm before they verged upon the trestle. She glanced fleetingly at Ki, seeing his reassuring smile, yet reading in his eyes a dismay she shared, a bitter regret that they had not caught the danger sooner. Fat chance. The setup aboard practically guaranteed that any warning would've come too late—short of Governor Cardwell's warning: "Never ride the train a-tall." And that one, she'd refused to heed.

The locomotive crested the brink, its leading truck jumping clear of the twisted rails. In the split second left before the train plummeted into the arroyo, Jessie was gripped fast, rooted with the irony of fate that neither she nor Cardwell, she felt sure, could've predicted back then in Tucson. His arguments against a train she hadn't yet seen had struck her as dark, mysterious, and hard to swallow. After all, she'd just arrived from a long, boring trip on the Southern Pacific Sunset Limited, and fully expected that the rest of her trip would be as uneventful, though hopefully cooler and a bit more entertaining. But what a difference a day made. . . . More than a day, actually, Jessie recalled as memories stabbed like lightning through her mind. The instant lingered, endlessly stretching. . . .

. . . Alighting at Tucson, Jessie and Ki felt the blast of direct afternoon sun as they hastened along the open track-bed to the depot. Inside, Ki set their bags down and dried his sweaty face with a large red bandanna, which Jessie wouldn't have minded trading for her lacy embroidered hanky, with which she was decorously if futilely daubing her perspiration.

To their relief, they would only have to roast in Tucson overnight. Tomorrow they'd be heading southwest for the Gila Mountains, to the construction site of the Blue River Dam, up by the old river-mining settlement of Whitewash. Plans were to visit briefly, detour down through Gila Basin, and return to her distant Circle Star ranch in Texas, ending an arduous round trip that Jessie didn't have to make. She wasn't summoned by a calamity; she had been invited to a ceremony marking completion of the dam's foundation. As sole heiress of the global Starbuck business empire, Jessie hadn't time to cover all the social and political requests she received, but she had an army of representatives and field operatives to cover such events or any other venture on her behalf.

Yet, like Alex Starbuck, her late father, Jessie had a desire and a knack for handling challenges — the contest of sharp dealing, the risk of high finance, the gamble of hunch-playing. So in this sense, Jessie knew that someone from Starbuck should go to Whitewash, but she was attending personally because she just plain felt like it.

If she didn't melt beforehand, she thought, eying her soggy handkerchief. "Maybe the Gila hills'll be cooler, maybe not," she predicted testily. "In any case, I've a suspicion it'll grow hotter before our trip's done."

"True enough," Ki agreed with a quiet smile. It was mid-June, yet the furnace of deep summer already baked the Southwest desert, and worse, an early hot spell like this was prone to take root, staying put and heating up. Picking up his small Gladstone and Jessie's leather bellows bag, Ki crossed the waiting room with Jessie falling in alongside. They barged outside and began to stride down the dusty street.

Tucson had an Indian heritage, with infusions of Spanish and *mestizo* blood. The result was a cluster of old, deteriorating adobe houses, rows of typical false-fronts, a smattering of tents and shanties, and one damn fool whose building had a galvanized tin roof. The few folks about moved according to where the shade was. Children, dogs, and goats hung around, brain-fried.

This made the stately, pseudo-Victorian Grand Union Continental Hotel where they were heading a unique and readily identifiable landmark. It was the finest and the newest, built when the Southern Pacific came through a couple of years before. It was convenient— merely four blocks from the depot—and it overlooked an expansive plaza of flat, bare cobbles and a horse-trough fountain.

Upon entering the lobby, Jessie and Ki were greeted effusively by the manager. He promptly gave their bags to a stooped, wizened old bellboy, then escorted them to the front desk. It was a deferential reception, which Jessie was used to, except the manager was laying on the smarm and bullshit overly thick, she thought.

Some of those who happened to be in the lobby just then gave the pair acknowledging nods and smiles. Those that weren't acquainted with them took discreet second glances, often as not at Jessie—the men admiring and the women envious of her striking beauty. Still in her twenties, she moved with lithe, regal grace, her taut, full breasts swelling her stylish two-piece outfit of light pearl-gray wool. Her leghorn hat hid the coils of her copper-blond tresses, but the hat's wide brim did little to conceal her cameo face, with its pert nose, dimpled chin, and audacious green eyes.

Equally intriguing was Ki. A lean-featured man with bronze skin, blue-black hair, and almond eyes, he exuded a magnetic quality that suggested he was capable of strong loyalty when it was earned, and unstoppable ferocity when he was provoked. Born to the Japanese wife of an American sailor, then orphaned as a boy in Japan, he'd been trained in martial arts and the other skills of a samurai. Though he packed no firearm, the waistcoat and pockets of his brown traveling suit carried short daggers and other small throwing-weapons, including the razor-sharp, star-shaped steel disks known as *shuriken*.

When Ki had first come to America, he'd placed his talents in the service of Alex Starbuck. Consequently, he and Jessie had virtually grown up together, and after

4

her father's murder, it seemed only fitting for him and Jessie to continue together. They were as affectionate and trusting as any blood-related brother and sister could be. They made a formidable team.

Reaching the desk, Jessie signed the register and was given her room key. Turning aside so Ki could sign in, she found herself cheek by jowl with the manager, who apologetically tugged his forelock.

"Miz Starbuck, ma'am, would you please accompany me?"

"Now? Where?"

"A private lounge. Mercy, that sounds dreadfully forward. I don't mean, I mean, I don't . . ." He swallowed, looking forlorn.

Ki stifled a grin. "Go ahead, Jessie. I'll see to your bag."

Nodding, Jessie beckoned for the manager to proceed. She walked with him through two large parlors that were sprinkled with hotel guests, and then down a central corridor almost to its end. The manager, halting, swept aside a scarlet drape which hung across the doorway and motioned for Jessie to go in.

As Jessie entered, the manager said, "May your visit be pleasant. Oh me, oh my." He released the drape, leaving Jessie alone in the room. There were no windows and the lamps were banked dim. It took a moment before her eyes adjusted to the darkness. Then she saw she was not alone. The dark outline of a middle-sized man stood to the side, in thick shadow. Other than that his right arm seemed to be in a sling, she could tell nothing about him. Toward the back, another man sat at an ornate round table, facing Jessie while reaching to turn up the milk-glass table lamp.

By the increased glow, she could see the man was in his mid-fifties, clad in a black Prince Albert with its single-breasted jacket unbuttoned and displaying a swath of white ruffle shirt. He was bald on top, sported

5

white muttonchops, had deceptively kindly grandpa eyes, and a bulbous nose that resembled the red bulb on a squeeze spray. Finishing any doubt Jessie had about who he was, he lit a fat torpedo cigar that stank uniquely like barbecued dog turds.

"Governor Cardwell! What on earth are you doing here?"

"Wishing the capital hadn't moved three y'ars ago from Tucson back to Prescott. Egad, it's a wretched piece to travel," he replied acerbically, puffing smoke. "Please, come sit."

"After you finish that cigar."

"Bad a vixen as ever, I swear." Chuckling, the Honorable David Lee Cardwell, Governor of Arizona Territory, crushed out his stogie as ordered.

Jessie sat facing him. She said warmly, "Well, this is a pleasure. But why the secrecy, your hiding away? Are you in danger?"

"Not a-tall. I simply wanted to talk with you privately. Can't set foot in the lobby without natterin' ninnies flocking around. Even m' cigars fail to roust 'em." Cardwell tapped his fingers thoughtfully. "You mightn't be so pleased when you hear me. I'll have to be brief, too, I fear. I'm catching your train westbound, and it's due out in less 'n an hour. Still, I won't be so blamed hurried I can't share a wee dram. A fine brandy, Miss Starbuck—if domestic. The new vineyards in northern California . . ."

Jessie nodded, the other man catching her eye now as he went to the sideboard along the left wall. His right arm was indeed in a sling—one of those big folded sheets that tie behind the neck; yet when he got out a cut-crystal decanter and three snifters, he moved slowly, deliberately, but never clumsily. He wore a black-and-white check cheviot suit and a string tie, and his black boots were shined glossy. But his coarse brown hair wouldn't stay combed; his face was weathered and seamed like arroyo country; and his wide-shouldered, bowlegged stance was that of a rangeman who looked as discomfited in his ill-suited suit as a goat in a gunnysack.

Cardwell began by easing in, digressing. "Before you arrived, I got to reflecting about when I met your dad, God rest him. 'Twas in '69, when the Whitewash environs were a-boom with placer mines, and Alex controlled a hefty share. At the peak of gold frenzy, he sold out, cash or trade, for Sulphur Spring Valley land. Everyone believed he'd bust a cog, and they took advantage, buying up his stocks, notes, mines, the works. Maybe I'd have too, if I hadn't been broke. Well, Alex left, and I needn't tell you who hooted last. Before year's end, Whitewash crashed, and until the dam, it was almost deserted, most of our mining coming from 'round Tombstone now." He smiled nostalgically. "I think Alex would've liked to see the developments there."

"Absolutely. I'm sure Father would've gone, for the same reason I am—to see what I can learn and adapt it for use in my areas. I also feel I'm going in his stead, in a sense. He was convinced he'd invested wisely in Sulphur Springs, that all it needed was water. When the dam is completed, it'll prove him right. It'll turn the whole Gila Basin from the arid wasteland it is now into a fertile belt for ranches and farms."

"Yes, it'll provide year-round irrigation and flood control. The dam will be a prestigious and economic achievement for the Territory, Miss Starbuck, and will certainly help Arizona attain statehood." Pausing as the man served them and sat down with his own drink, Cardwell then introduced him. "Jessica Starbuck, Marshal Ross Ulrich. Ross is the law o'er Bonita way, on loan to me, sort of," he told Jessie, and left it at that as he went on: "Have you seen the train leaving tomorrow to the dam site? No? Take my word, you'll ride a war

7

surplus coach tacked onto the regular rattler for the construction crews and supplies, a rolling pigsty on a short-line of unsafe equipment and slap-dash trackage. It'd be a rude dose of misery and possible mishap for a pretty young lady who—and please, don't take me wrong, don't misconstrue my intent—who isn't an Arizonan with vested interests."

Astonished, Jessie took a sip of brandy, then replied, "Thanks for your warning. I might've thought you were saying that tripe I was mishearing. Of course you want me to go. You put me on your personal invitation list, along with the other interested parties I'll meet here tonight or on the train tomorrow."

"On the infernal train," Cardwell echoed glumly. "With a hundred and fifty thousand dollars, may I add, plus guards. The next major phase of the dam is to begin once that money is deposited in the Whitewash bank for workers' pay and materials." He waved a hand dismissively. "Please. For your sake, for the sake of Alex's memory, for the sake of my conscience. Don't go."

"Whyever not?"

"I'd rather not say."

"Then you know my answer, Governor."

"Same as Alex's would've been. Like father, like daughter—like obstinate blue-faced mules. So much for my druthers. Miss Starbuck, from the reports I've been getting, we seem to be fighting the ghosts of Whitewash Cemetery."

"Ghosts! There aren't such things as ghosts."

"Impossible or not, there's a reign of terror in Whitewash which, if unchecked, will stop the dam from being built."

Marshal Ulrich spoke up then, in a flinty voice. "The locals swear it's 'cause of the dam. When it's completed, its back-up waters will inundate the cemetery, which's in a small valley slightly west of Whitewash.

It's more like a big ol' burial ground, actually, first used by the Indians and later by the miners from around the region. Superstition has it that the ground must be left undisturbed."

"A common belief among Indians and the uneducated," Jessie remarked.

"Yeah, and most of the locals are just that—uneducated. The smart ones left after the gold dried up, and are either in the Gila Basin, below the town, or where mining has been proved profitable. But even so, it still don't account for the appearance of mysterious skeleton riders swoopin' out of the graveyard, burnin' and ravagin' surroundin' homes and the dam site, and, I'm afraid, even killin'."

"Now understand, I don't believe in ghosts any more than you do," Cardwell declared flatly. "When I heard of this foofaraw, I dispatched two top lawmen to Whitewash. One was shot dead."

"The other was shot almost dead," Ulrich added with grim irony, and motioned with his right arm.

Jessie frowned and leaned on the table. "Tell me about the ghosts, Marshal—particularly any you might've seen."

Sliding the milk-glass lamp over a little, Marshal Ulrich regarded Jessie with a serious countenance, and related his run-in with the ghosts. "It wasn't very late at night, but there wasn't a moon and it was overcast to boot, so it was pretty dang dark. I was returning from scouting about when I passed within hailin' distance of the McGeephers' homestead, and since their lamp was still burning and my gut was a-growlin', I gave 'em a hail. The door flung open and McGeephers came out, armed. But we got that straightened out and I got inside."

Ulrich, continuing, described the cabin's main room as spartan, bare of everything except a stone fireplace and heavy working-gear and the absolute essentials for living. There was a bedroom off to one side, shrouded by a blanket stretched across the doorway, but Ulrich was positive there wasn't any trickery in there, or much of anything else. Mrs. McGeephers was cooking at the hearth, within sight the whole time. After an initial reticence, Ol' Man McGeephers was warmly opinionating on the subject of ghosts. He believed in 'em.

When Ulrich had asked McGeephers if he thought the local nightriders hid out at the cemetery, Ulrich quoted McGeephers as answering, "'I don't think it. I know it. The lay of my land makes it a handy cross-country route for the cemetery, and I seen 'em plenty comin' and goin' on their raids in the Basin. They're visible, flickering' and dancin' with that glow of theirs plumb up to the graveyard, and there they just vanish. I knowed. I follered 'em.'"

Then, according to Ulrich, they heard a soft scraping noise just outside the window. He spun around. McGeephers lifted his head. They both stared at the apparition they saw. Ulrich never considered himself superstitious, and would've laughed if he'd been told this. But there was no denying his eyes, not when all three inside saw the same thing.

Through the hazy, smoke-filmed glass was the pale outline of a glowing skeleton, topped by a death's-head with firebrand sockets for eyes, its fleshless mouth ripped back in a wild, demoniacally fiendish grin. One bony hand could also be seen, clutching in its shining claw the handle of a revolver—a revolver whose giant bore was aiming directly at McGeephers. Ulrich desperately threw himself sideways into McGeephers, just as the revolver in the skeletal figure's hand spat flame.

The shattering crash of window glass commingled with the reverberating report of the pistol, filling the room with sound and smoke as Ulrich and McGeephers struck the floor, with Mrs. McGeephers a screaming step away. The bullet caught Ulrich in the bicep, nicking his armbone on its way through. There was another shot fired from the window, and then the raider disappeared, its macabre laughter floating on the wind behind it.

As Mrs. McGeephers bustled to get old cloths for bandages, McGeephers was trying to get Ulrich's jacket off, and Ulrich was fountaining blood while fumbling for a left-handed hold on his pistol. It was then that the ghosts reappeared outside the window, just long enough to pitch blazing torches through the opening. The whole front room burst into bright, licking flames. Smoke billowed, choking them. With Ulrich forced to grip his arm to staunch the flow of blood, the McGeephers had to help him out the door, hardly much better off than an invalid. Stumbling into the front yard, a salvo of bullets sent them scurrying for cover behind the farm wagon, which was drawn under a cottonwood growing off to the left.

The farmyard around them was like a scene from some vivid nightmare—though to Ulrich what he saw was all-too-terrible reality. The spectral figures of the raiders were tearing wildly about the blackened grounds, screaming banshee sounds that shattered the night into broken fragments.

Some held burning torches in their bony hands, and even as Ulrich and the McGeephers watched, helpless, pinned down by the sporadic fire of the other raiders, the barn and the livestock pens and the small lean-to for horses were set afire. Flames leapt high into the black sky, destroying what it had taken the McGeephers years of toil to build. When the raiders had completed their grisly task, they banded together at the entrance lane to the McGeephers farm, still sending salvos of shots at the wagon, preventing the defenders from returning fire except intermittently and without aim.

Then, as if from the depths of whatever hell had

11

spawned the ghosts, as one they chorused a hollow, chilling laugh that Ulrich admitted curdled his marrow. They spurred their horses along the lane, their spectral bodies glowing dancing light in the darkness.

Ulrich and the McGeephers came out from their concealment, and Mrs. McGeephers used Ulrich's shirt to bind his wound there. Then they stood in a slump-shouldered, dejected group, all the buildings around them blazing infernos of flame and black smoke—the dream of an industrious couple dying in fanning, searing heat. Ulrich felt sick about it, too. And useless.

Mrs. McGeephers lamented, "They finished us off, just like they done lots of others in Gila Basin the past few weeks." And old McGeephers agreed, adding, "They've burned us out complete, Ma." Ulrich had thought furiously for anything, however slight, that wasn't so totally gloomy and depressing. . . .

Now, gazing at Jessie, Ulrich said, "Well, ma'am, I came up with something. I looked at the McGeephers and told 'em, 'At least we know thems ain't ghosts. No ghosts tote shootin' irons. You mark my words: Flesh an' blood are behind this here raiding and killing, and whoever it be, there's bound to be some low-down reason behind it, too.'" Ulrich sighed. "But McGeephers said he wasn't stayin' to test my notions, and once he was gone, wild horses couldn't drag him back. And I'm afraid his opinion is echoed by many, maybe most, of the workers at the dam. They're threatening to leave, and if they go, the dam is finished before it's started."

Jessie sat back in her chair, perturbed. The dam was one of the most important projects in the territory. It was sorely needed by the farmers and ranchers of Gila Basin, and by Arizonans as a whole in their bid for statehood. If the dam failed because of ghostly midnight raiders, it would turn Arizona into the laughingstock of the nation, and the Congress would think the Southwest was inhabited by silly, ignorant children unfit to govern themselves. Failure of the dam was worse than having no dam begun! And yet—it sounded impossible.

"I don't believe it," she said, shaking her head. "I won't believe it until I see these ghosts myself, and I know very well I never will. There has to be a mundane reason for it all."

"You're going to get that chance, Miss Starbuck," Cardwell said, "if you insist on ignoring my personal and professional advice to stay here. If you must go to Whitewash, be aware that circumstances may be delicate as well as dangerous. You'll be traveling with a select group—some very influential, some having authority, some rich and some with it all. If they return with stories of ghosts roaming the night, we will be in serious trouble. And I'm sure you understand that if I was directly involved publicly, it'd only add to an already untenable situation."

"I understand."

The governor suddenly looked up, over Jessie's shoulder. When Jessie turned, she saw the manager standing in the doorway.

"I must leave now," Cardwell said, rising. "I'm sorry I can't persuade you to remain here safe, but I'm pleased we had this time together. Forewarned is forearmed." He smiled, though it was a weary and saddened expression. "Good luck, Miss Starbuck . . . and *watch out*."

Chapter 2

Watch out, Jessie repeated to herself, as Cardwell's parting caveat flickered through her thoughts.

She had taken the governor's final warning as she had taken much of the rest—with skepticism. And considering it now, she remembered her facetious tone when relating the confab to Ki. He hadn't known what to make of it, aside from not making a joke of it, and had assumed a wait-and-see attitude. He'd remained non-committal most of the way, most of the time, right up to here—a moment ago, when he was blasted smack dab into this mess, shouting: *"Watch out!"* An intriguing turn, that, looping around myriad images . . . a circle of flashbacks sparking kaleidoscopic in Jessie's mind eye . . .

. . . A red moon hung over the Gila Mountains. In its baleful rays, the Blue River became a stream of blood flowing between banks of jet. Far to the north, looming peaks curved eastward to the yonder San Franciscos and

15

Mogollon Rim. The massed rimline towered against a blue-black sky which was dusty with stars. Nearer, broken foothills pitched south and west, staggered in rangeland steppes, slashing the desert with their iron claws.

From the base of the hills stretched parched corrugations, dry of life, stunted of growth. Due west lay the San Carlos Indian Reservations. Southward, the dusty flats of Gila Basin spread to Sulphur Spring Valley, in between the stony Peloncillo Range and the Pinaleno Mountains on the west.

Shrouded by night the trackless reaches blurred, obscure, a purple mystery flecked with silver ash. The opposite extreme had hit about twelve hours earlier, when the daylight exposed the lowlands full on, in starker relief and for a longer time than anyone cared to endure, as the train from Tucson steamed for the hills across the sun-bleached wilderness.

Jessie was gratified that that section was over. They'd been laboring up through the hills since twilight, and now a bloodshot moon was out. But the night and the climb and wide-open windows didn't seem to cut the heat one degree. She glanced at Ki, who was seated alongside. They exchanged quiet smiles, both feeling drained of idle talk. She sat back then, closing her eyes and fanning her face with an old copy of *Harper's Bazaar*.

Shifting, Ki leaned staring out the window to catch more breeze, and to discourage anyone prowling for conversation. By nature a taciturn man, Ki had sided Jessie and met the other members of her ceremonial delegation, but joined in the palaver only minimally. He'd found most of the delegates to be budding politicos of one type or another—a lawyer from Phoenix, a councilman from Tempe, a large landowner from Flagstaff —and while they were all decent, dedicated men in their way, their way tended toward dudin' up stuffy and bombasting pompous. Although Jessie lost marks for being a "fe-male," she still had more in common with them than Ki did. At least, handling boiled collars and gasbags was more in her line.

Besides the delegation, the train was carrying a small crew, some dam laborers up in a forward crewcar, and ten or so paying passengers in the coach. These folks came as a surprise to the delegates, and Ki suspected they may've come illegally. Like most private shortlines, this one was likely limited to the dam project, and prohibited from hauling all else. But area locals needed a rail link and the train crew could use the pocket money, so naturally the coach would get pressed into regular irregular service. The power of American free enterprise won again.

There was also another reason why Ki kept his face poking out the window. Jessie had reported the coach might be war surplus; he believed it, suspecting the War of 1812, by its decrepitude. It had a musty reek as if it had once sunk in naval action, too. Mingling unpleasantly were smells of current use, of sulphurous locomotive smoke, of bananas peddled by a news butcher in Tucson, of the chewing tobacco splashed on the rims of its iron cuspidors, of shelled peanuts, whiskey hip-flasks, cigars, and pipes. All-pervasive like a miasma wafted the rank, ripe odors of sweat. Bodies, clothes, washed, dirty, all sweaty.

Now Ki abruptly became aware of a new and strange and pleasing fragrance, the perfume of frangipani. He turned from the window. Kid-gloved hands clinging to the grimy seatbacks for support, a young woman was advancing along the swaying aisle. Her flowered foulard skirt swept the cindery floor. A parasol, looped to her wrist, brushed a delegate's arm as she passed. A huge bow of crushed strawberry silk formed a sort of bustle at her hips, accentuating the fact she had a leanthighed, pert-breasted figure that intimated a sly sensuality.

When she reached Jessie, the girl settled on the empty reverse seat directly across and regarded her with hazel eyes. Twenty, Jessie estimated; a year or two either side, no more. And quite pretty, with a snub-nosed oval face, a full mouth that was almost too wide, and a loose bun of coiled auburn hair. But her eyes were her dominant feature, having character—brooding and moist, like light brown olives.

Jessie smiled politely. It seemed to encourage the girl, who asked in a clear if hesitant voice, "Are you Miss Starbuck? With the delegation to the Blue River dam?" When Jessie nodded, the girl chippered. "Oh, good. I'd be awfully embarrassed if I were wrong. My name is Diedre Maddox, Miss Starbuck—"

"Please, call me Jessie." She introduced Ki.

After a word or two of small talk, Ki bowed out of their conversation and turned to the window. The train was following a ridgeline, and he could see a vista now, with long slopes swelling toward rounded hilltops. Below dropped sharply out of his view, but he judged it to be perhaps five hundred feet down. By craning, he could see the gleam of tracks ahead and behind where they vanished around shoulders of the hills, and as the train curved, he caught a glimpse ahead of a steep, boulder-strewn, brushy slope, and a long trestle spanning a deep, wide arroyo. From behind him came snatches of chatter:

". . . I live in Whitewash. More properly, down in Gila Basin on the Slash-C—C for Caleb Maddox, my father. One of the best and biggest ranches around, if I may say so," Diedre was telling Jessie. "Well, the last years I spent mainly at college in Albuquerque, but I've graduated now, and'll live at home—and do what I can about these ghost raiders. You know about our ghosts, I suppose?"

"I've heard," Jessie hedged. "Have you mentioned them to others?"

"If you mean the delegates, heavens no. I wouldn't wish to *impose* on the men, or be patted on the head and sent off to find a husband. I feel much more confident now, talking woman to woman. What do you think? You don't believe in them, do you?"

"Who, men?"

"Ghosts."

"No, I don't."

"Well, neither do I," Diedre stated firmly. There was something that might have been fear and pain in her eyes now, and bitterness was in her voice when she continued. "I think the raids and the killings are the work of real men. And I . . . I fear my Uncle Genesee may be involved with them."

Jessie took a deep breath and smiled lightly. "I appreciate your trust, but please be careful. A word overheard, or confided to the wrong person has led to lynchings, vendettas, tragedies galore. Now, why do you suspect your uncle?"

"How he acts, his attitudes. He's changed since I made him ranch manager last fall, when Dad died. I felt lucky to have someone to run it, and he'd worked for Dad two, three months by then, so I left Uncle in charge while I finished college, like Dad wished. Now, he's doing okay as manager. But *being* manager, the head honcho, I think has fattened his head."

"That may be, Diedre, but what's the link to the raiders?"

"Links, Miss St—Jessie: First, Uncle Genesee turned against the dam project. He quarrels and scuffles, too, according to friends' letters. He argues the dam'll let area nesters wax bigger, and'll draw hordes more riffraff, causing rack and ruin to us and other large ranches. He's just parroting the big stockmen he chums with, who goad him into messes as a joke." Diedre shook her head sadly. "Trouble is, they believe their own guff. They feel threatened. When rich established gentry band to act, it's with the power they respect, not the law they've helped subvert. The Tonto Basin sheep feud. Acorn Hole squatter fight. They do it themselves, or hire it done. Like the Colfax Country range war, where the stockmen deputized outlaws to wipe out the shoestring cow outfits."

"Is that your opinion, Diedre? The raiders are killers hired to play ghosts, and your uncle and these stockmen are behind it?"

Before Diedre could reply, the train lurched around a sharp curve.

Ki could see ahead to the trestle that spanned the wide arroyo. He heard Diedre begin her answer: "I fear, Jessie, I fear..." as his peering eyes noted a swirl of blue smoke trickling from up the end of the trestle. "Uncle tags after them, up over his head, but he won't be let into their secrets. They'll throw him the short end of the stick—"

"Hey!" Ki exclaimed, "looks like there's a fire on the trestle. Can't be much of it, though, by the looks of the smoke—*Watch out!*"

From the end of the trestle burst an earsplitting concussion, a blinding flash of orange light and acrid black smoke. Hurtling through the tumbling masses flew crossties, fractured beam ends, and metal shards.

The next instant, glittering fans of sparks showered from the locomotive wheels as airbrakes ground in a panicked emergency stop. The five cars of the train's "bobtail" had only individual mechanical brakes, as best Ki could tell; instead of a clamping grind of shoes and a thumping of brake rigging along the length of the cars, there was a prodigious hammering of couplers. The locomotive bucked, leaped like a living thing, slowed almost instantly, then surged ahead again under the piledriver slam of the cars.

The white-faced fireman crouched on the lowest cab-step, leaning. Then he took a deep breath and vaulted far out from the rocketing engine. With the pilot of the locomotive reaching for the brink of the arroyo, the engineer hurled himself through the cab window. Past him howled the vainly braking locomotive with bellowing bell-stack and grinding drivers, and a captive string of rolling stock shoving to the twisted end of the rails—and beyond.

Arcing, the locomotive rammed the rocky far bank with a crushing impact. But for the drag of the baggage car, locomotive and tender would have somersaulted completely. The beginning of a semi-somersault yanked the baggage car and the front end of the crew car clear of the rail. The baggage car telescoped the tender and crunched into the stony bed of the arroyo.

Instead of telescoping, the remaining cars jack-knifed. The forward end of the crew car was jerked high in the air by the half-somersault of the baggage car. As the coupling snapped, the boxcar following sideswiped the upended crew car and slewed it about. An instant later the crew car slammed down on the loose rocks of the railroad embankment, rolled over, and came to rest on its side against a line of boulders at the arroyo's bank.

The fourth car, another boxcar, smashed sidewise into the rear end of the tender, jammed it into the arroyo bed almost atop the crewcab, then crashed bottom-up, crosswise of the track at the edge of the demolished trestle. The front truck of the last car, the coach, remained on the rails, but its rear end, like the cracker of a whip, was spun about, and it wrenched the truck loose. Slewing about in the air, the coach overturned and plunged with a thunderous splintering of its wooden frame, and came to rest, slanting overturned against the locomotive.

To Jessica, dazed and struggling, caught in the debris

of the coach, it seemed as if her eardrums were about to burst from the noise, as if the sound of the collision continued on and on, maddeningly. Ki, stunned asprawl nearby, was also unaware that the deafening din was caused by the steam escaping from the boiler of the ruptured locomotive. It had drowned out the screams, the crackle of rending, shattering wood, even the crash of the coach as it came to rest next to the locomotive.

Ki's body throbbed with bruising pain, but he felt no major agonies. His head pulsed with a dull ache as, reviving, he fought from beneath the bench seats, paneling, and cushions that buried him. The coach was a shambles. Everything that had been attached had broken loose, and everything already loose had been flung about looser, then tossed upside down to pile up in the trough of the sloping roof. Overhead he could see segments of night sky through the broken floorboarding, while all around, the uninjured passengers were hysterical to abandon ship, a-bellow with yells and squawks as they scrambled across the jumble and dove out the broken windows. Wreathing everything was foggy steam.

Wriggling free, Ki twisted about. There was no sign of Diedre, and he assumed she'd escaped outside. Of Jessie, only her arm was visible; she was entombed under an avalanche of overhead racks, burst cushions, suitcases, a cuspidor, splintered wood, and twisted metal. Furiously he began digging down around her, flinging debris about. He asked, "Are you okay? Broken? What?"

"Okay, I think," she replied, her voice muffled. "I'm pinned or hooked on something, and I can't break loose."

"Maybe I can haul you out," he said. Then he abruptly stiffened, something having caught his eye from outside the coach. He turned his head, staring through the row of smashed windows, and in that moment he saw some dozen separate, eerily wavering glows bunched close together. They were approaching from the brush that flanked the arroyo bed, flickering spectrally in the red-moon night, blearing in the mists forming inside the coach.

Jessie called; "What's wrong? What is it?"

"Visitors, the ones you've asked to meet. Pull with me." Seizing Jessie's arm, Ki lunged backward while applying hard yet straight and consistent pressure, struggling to drag her free without wrenching her muscles or snapping her bones. He succeeded in tugging her head and shoulders from beneath the pile, but one leg remained trapped.

Still, by craning she could now glimpse the ghostly shapes that were converging upon them. As she worked with Ki, frantic to break out, they could see skeletonlike features and outlines, gleaming bones, and leering, hideous skulls. Folks outside who'd bawled to flee the wreckage were bleating to get under cover. Drowning them out in a sudden explosion, a barrage of gunfire ripped from the spirit attackers, peppering the broken train inside and out around, callously indifferent whether they struck fear or flesh.

Trying to ignore the shots whipping and ricocheting through the coach, Ki yanked aside more seat cushions only to discover that the jagged end of a fractured wooden beam had been driven through a partition underneath Jessie. The combination effectively stapled her in place. Prying, thrusting against the beam, he jogged it aside sufficiently to release her, then helped her crawl free. For a brief moment she hunkered, glimpsing several of the silvery forms running toward the baggage car under cover fire from their cohorts. The baggage car lay crumpled and ruptured, its windows smashed, its sliding doors wrenched partially open and jammed in their slots by the terrific impact.

"The money!" Jessie exclaimed, striking across the clutter. There was not much she or Ki could do, she had

23

to admit; for all practical purposes they were pinned down like everyone else. She hoped the four armed guards entrenched with the money in the baggage car would be able to stop them.

Ki caught up, and together they forged for the nearest vestibule. The intolerable screaming of escaping steam had not lessened as they scrambled over debris on hands and knees; the noise dampened the sporadic gunfire blasting outside. The ghostly killers had been retiring to the brushy thickets and were firing from within, their eerie luminosity making them look like flitting fireflies in the protective growth.

Then suddenly there was a tremendous echoing eruption, and the night sky was lit brightly from the direction of the baggage car. Jessie felt the solid, jarring impact underfoot, and knew immediately that powder had been used to blow open the baggage car. She heard Ki curse softly but vehemently, provoked by his helpless frustration. Bullets whined over and around them. There came more rapid gunfire from the baggage car, and then all fell quiet . . . for a moment. Then another detonation seared the night, a smaller one this time.

Reaching the vestibule, they crept outside, wary of drawing gunfire, and eased toward the baggage car using whatever cover they could find. The car lay on the other side of the locomotive, and coming abreast of the point where the coach grazed up against the locomotive, they could see scalding steam pouring into the shattered windows.

It was then that they glimpsed five spectral figures rushing toward the brush. Then the shooting ceased altogether. Hoofbeats replaced the pistol and rifle fire, retreating rapidly, and they could see the ghostly killers hightailing to the arroyo, the flickering phosphorescence growing smaller until once again there was only a bunched series of dancing glows fading up the crevice.

Train crew, laborers, locals, and delegates, all the

able-bodied were rising from their scattered shelter in and out about the strewn wreckage. A bubbling ferment of shouting and questioning, stirred with gesticulating, spilled boiling while they crowded at the baggage car and trampled around the other cars.

Jessie and Ki failed to locate Diedre among the survivors.

So far there was no sign of fire or smoke, and the thundering roar of the escaping steam was subsiding a little. The locomotive engineer grew impatient and began shouting commands, waving his arms and pointing, bringing order out of chaos. More than a dozen injured, including a remarkably few gunshot-wounded, were deposited downstream along both banks. Crushed legs, compound fractures, and puncture wounds lay asprawl. One man, face down, was digging his fingers spasmodically into the gravelly dirt. Another was rolling his head from side to side, biting colorless lips to fight back cries of pain. A third lay motionless, eyes half open, oblivious to the flies crawling across his face.

Diedre was not among this group either.

Returning to the coach, Jessie and Ki were scanning the smashed exterior while approaching the vestibule entry when they heard the locomotive engineer yelling at them to stop. Jessie made the error of hesitating to see what was the matter.

"You can't go in there!" the engineer insisted, taking her by the arm.

"But there's a girl missing. We think she may still be in there."

"No, no, you two were the last ones out. The steam will blind you now!"

"Don't worry," Ki called, ducking into the vestibule. "I won't go up the flue."

Despite the open windows, the opaque clouds of steam hovered, thick and cloying, in the car. Ki stumbled along, a protecting arm shielding his face as he peered around. Ahead, almost to the scalding water leaking from the locomotive's boiler, in rubble largely hidden by wraith-like streamers of steam, his eye caught a splotch of bright color. It was, he saw, a crumpled mass of strawberry ostrich tips on a black straw hat with a silk lining of crushed strawberry. The whole thing was stirring feebly.

He needed no second glance at the disarrayed length of flowered foulard to know it was Diedre Maddox. He plunged deeper into the seething steam, pressing his kerchief to his mouth so he wouldn't inhale the burning mist. He found Diedre prone in the midst of steam-soaked seat cushions, stirring feebly, an iron baggage rack wedged across her back.

He toppled the wreckage aside, and was reaching to help Diedre up when she moaned woozily. "Broken, I imagine. Right leg is broken."

"Well, we'll move you somehow. You can't stay here."

"I got here a lot quicker. Flew. Landed conk on my noggin, and when I came to, everyone'd gone and I couldn't crawl out." Gamely, Diedre tried to get up, but grimaced and fell back when she put weight on her right foot.

The crushed-strawberry parasol still dangled from her wrists. Breathing through the balled kerchief now clamped between his teeth, Ki ripped ribs and fabric from the handle. Diedre clenched her jaw as he wrapped the parasol handle against her leg with the rib-supported fabric and bound it in place with strips from the parasol.

The air close to the inverted ceiling was reasonably free of steam. Her face showed no trace of scalding, and he doubted she had drawn any steam into her lungs. On hands and knees, Ki dragged her toward the vestibule as gently as the circumstances permitted. Once in the vestibule he faced the problem of lifting her over the curved gable of the overturned coach. He climbed outside, gulped down a deep breath of fresh air, bent over the obstruction and shouted to Diedre to lock her arms about his neck. She gasped in pain once, when her ankle collided with the obstruction, but otherwise made no protest.

Carrying Diedre to a grassy patch, Ki eased her to the ground and knelt to examine her right leg with analyzing fingers. The ankle was swollen, the skin unbroken. "It might be a simple fracture," he told her. "But my guess is it's more likely a bad sprain."

Jessie came over with the engineer, who clapped a heavy hand on Ki's shoulder. "Nice work, pal. I reckon that about accounts for everybody."

"Well, everybody better keep their eyes open and their guns handy. I doubt those hellions'll come back, but it doesn't pay to take chances with a bunch like that."

"They'll get a hot reception if they do," the engineer promised grimly. "My fireman is up tapping into the telegraph line now, and there'll be a rescue party out here afore long, I 'spect. P'raps come with a posse, too, though it's too late now. Them cussed Death Riders got what they was after."

Nodding, Ki glanced across at the baggage car, which was silent and shadowy, and had a gaping hole where its doors had been. The four guards had been taken out, dead; those who had not been killed by the powder blast had been shot in cold blood by the spectral raiders. The safe was empty. The hundred and fifty thousand dollars earmarked for the Blue River dam construction was gone.

Chapter 3

The rescue train from Whitewash was a grungy string of boxcars and flats pulled by an aged saddleback switcher. By the time it showed, everybody was impatiently waiting up trackside, along with the dead and injured, and a goodly amount of recovered belongings. The night was passing 2 A.M. when finally they reached the town depot, accompanied by the local sheriff, a doctor, and some volunteers who'd gone along to help.

The confusion was great. Despite the late hour, they were met by a noisy pack of locals and construction workers, swarming mostly from the saloons. A few were fancily dressed and sober, indicating they were the Prominent Citizens on hand to greet the ceremonial delegation. And despite their exhaustion, the delegates fulminated, outraged, while the other passengers blistered the air blue with tales of their ordeal.

Much of their hue and cry was directed at Sheriff Beard, just as it had been upon his arrival at the wreck. He listened to the complainers with a grumpy face more wrinkled and battered than the Big Four Stetson he wore, a gnarled hand resting on the worn plow-handle of his low-holstered revolver. Meanwhile, paunch-bellied Ol' Doc Terwilliger was loudly directing the removal of the injured to the Rosebud Hotel, next to his home clinic, but otherwise he ignored the mob, a somewhat dyspeptic look on his bejowled features.

Jessie and Ki got off with their luggage, then helped Diedre down. She had only a hatbox left, having shipped everything else in trunks, which had been demolished in the baggage car explosion. Her ankle was now tightly bandaged, wrapped by the doctor when he'd diagnosed it as badly sprained; she favored it, limping as they began edging through the hubbub.

"I've still quite a ride to the Slash-C," she remarked, "and I'm dead tired. I think I'll see if the hotel can put me up."

Suddenly a hoarse shout called, "Diedre! There you are!"

She turned, startled, and gasped, "Charlie!"

A young man hastened towards them, shouldering through the crowd. He appeared to be in his mid-twenties, gangly, clad in dungarees and a plaid shirt, and a belly nutria Montana which he swept off as he approached. His shiny black hair was cropped very short, resembling the way men were barbered in prison. "I heard tell you was comin' back t'day, Diedre. And yuh was on this train! Great Gawd!"

Abruptly, she seemed to remember that his eyes were not the only ones on her. "How are you, Charlie?" she asked in polite conversational tones. "It's nice to see you again, even under such unusual circumstances."

Then a gruffer voice snapped, "Git away, Wolfe!" Another, older man appeared out of the crowd, indignation evident in his ruddy complexion.

Heedless, Charlie Wolfe asked Diedre anxiously, "Leg hurt? You aw'ri'?"

"Just took a sprain and a bad scare, Charlie, but maybe it's best—"

"Git, jailbird, git goin'! Ain't you damaged the lady enough?"

"—if you went," she finished, patting his arm. "We can talk later."

"Yeah, sure." As Wolfe grudgingly turned away, he spit a thin stream of brown tobacco juice, narrowly missing the other man's boots. "Sorry, Shylock, but hell, yuh got fellers to lick 'em clean," he sneered, stalking off.

And Diedre lashed out, "How dare you interfere, Mr. Hevis!"

The man named Hevis spluttered, disconcerted. "Why, I was only considering your interests, Diedre. We must stand firm against such rogues." Fortyish, he was spare, straight-featured, with steadfast eyes and a righteous mouth, and wearing a sack-style dark suit with a starched shirt and a derby hat. He added, in an excuse loudly aimed at the sheriff, "It's high time a little gumption arose in Whitewash. The Southeastern Cattleman's Exchange and Trust Bank faces a great loss because of the robbery tonight."

"Lucian!" Sheriff Beard yelled in reply. "Lucian, that money didn't belong to your bank. You were only going to store it here a spell."

"Arnold Beard, you old fool," Hevis called back. "We hold notes and mortgages on the nesters in the Basin. Without the dam, they won't have water to raise crops and livestock, resulting in bankruptcies and foreclosures. The bank needs interest off the loans, and fat, prosperous customers, not tracts of worthless land. We all need you to bring in the desperados."

"Bring 'em in? I can't get within shootin' distance, blast it! We chase 'em when able, but most of us including me are sorta new up here, and them faceless lobos must know every hole an' sidecut in the district. Anyhow, they wind up at the same place, the graveyard. I've been out there a dozen times since the trouble started, and that's where the trail always ends!"

Leaving the two men haranguing each other, Jessie, Ki, and an annoyed but silent Diedre headed up the main street. On their right, the bordering railroad track ran on into the hills to the yonder dam site. Along their left stretched the town's buildings, some of which had reopened since Whitewash's revival, others still being restored, and a few remaining abandoned derelicts, innards stripped, tangles of brush and trash piled against their sagging walls.

The Rosebud Hotel & Club was housed in a freshly painted and refurbished two-story falsefront. Light glowed through a facade of frosted glass windows. The inside, they found, was rather congested, and vibrant with voices. They joined the flock clamoring for rooms at the nearby registration desk, and while working up in turn, they had time to look around.

Except for delegates holding reservations, the folks besieging the hotel were like Diedre, caught out late and hoping to lay over. Others, mostly dam laborers, ranch hands and farm hands and the ilk, were making a night of it at the far, club end of the open post-and-beam interior. The long, mirror-blazing bar was lined with customers, several poker games were in play, and chuck-a-luck and roulette tables were operating. The dance floor and dining table area had been cleared for the train wreck victims, who lay in rows on bedding while the doctor and a bevy of bar belles administered aid.

Gradually the three pressed closer, while a harried clerk scudded from patron to patron as if blown by the wind, gray whiskers fanning out on his wizened face. Helping whenever possible was the busy owner, a tall and leonine man in his mid-thirties, who moved agilely and efficiently, rushing without seeming frazzled or frantic. He happened to be there when Jessie and Ki signed for their booked rooms, and Diedre asked for any available bedspace.

The clerk shook his head. "Nary a cot nor cranny left."

"Take mine," Ki said, handing her his key.

The owner declared "Now, there's a gent" before Diedre could object, and glancing from the register to Ki, he continued, "Name's Ki, eh? Listen, I suppose you could use Emile Gothe's bunk, if you don't mind some muss. My best dealer, but he didn't show up last night and hasn't shown today, either."

"Where'd he go, Mist' Chenault?" the clerk asked, locating a spare key.

"Who knows? Who can tell about dealers, or gamblers of any stripe? Here today, gone tomorrow. I run straight games, but maybe someplace before, Emile got caught cold-deckin' or with a sleeve clip. Dealers lam out then, those who can, and if the past catches up, they lam again. That's my guess, someone who knew him chancing into town and Emile vamoosing pronto." Chenault, the owner, shrugged, unconcerned. "Whatever, I don't expect to see him back again."

Ki nodded, thanking Chenault, then started up the stairs with Jessie and Diedre. Jessie paused at one point to glance back down at Chenault, impressed. Unlike the oily gamblers and thuggish pimps who plied this business, he struck her as reasonably genuine, diligent, and honest, displaying consideration to Ki and compassion for the injured. And he had those handsome Gallic features that seemed to promise merry sinning....

After seeing the women safely ensconced in their rooms, Ki found Emile Gothe's room at the end of the rear corridor. It was very small, tidy in the way card manipulators often are, with its one window ajar for air and overlooking a scruffy tree. The narrow bed sagged when he sat down. It hit bottom on something, so he

33

peered underneath. Then he got up, went out, locking the door, and returned to the lobby.

"I found him," he reported. "A lump under the bed."

Chenault regarded him dubiously. "You sure tied a load on in a hurry, Ki. Who's under your bed—a boa constrictor or a pink elephant?"

"Emile Gothe, with a knife in his chest. In his room."

"That's the last place anybody ever searches when one of those pasteboard shufflers show up missin'," Chenault complained. He turned to the clerk. "You hustle down and notify the sheriff. Tell him we'll be in Emile's room."

Emile Gothe did not make a pretty corpse. His shirt was crusted with dried blood and his limbs were contorted, and on his dead face was frozen a peculiar expression.

"Looks like he was more startled than scared," Ki noted.

"I guess it came as a shock to find himself dead," Chenault remarked. "Well, this leaves me short a dealer —right before payday at the dam. Blazes! Ever deal cards?"

"Afraid my hand isn't up to snuff for a place like yours," Ki replied, smiling. "How about your clerk?"

"That ol' hellion couldn't get his hand into a barrel without bustin' a stave. All he's good for is to deal 'em off the bar to his mouth."

"That's a lie," the clerk protested, suddenly appearing with Sheriff Beard. "I eat, too."

"Not if you've a chance to drink instead. Hello, Sheriff."

"Howdy. See business is keepin' up." Beard clumped into the room, while behind at the doorway grew a cluster of curious hotel guests, including Jessie and Diedre. Glancing up from the body, he asked, "Who done him in, Neal?"

"Dunno," Chenault answered, shrugging. "Emile was missing last night, and he looks to've been dead that long. His door was locked, so we used our spare key to look in, but we never spotted him under the bed, an' figured he'd skipped out. This feller here, Ki, he found Emile just now when I lent him the room to bunk in."

The sheriff eyed Ki sternly. "Weren't you on the train, too?"

"Yeah. I didn't wreck it, either."

"Remains to be seen. And speakin' of seein' remains..." Sheriff Beard proceeded to go through the dead man's pockets, unearthing a miscellany of articles and a considerable amount of money. "Robbery wasn't the motive, anyhow." A moment later he drew forth Gothe's room key. "And it 'pears the killer didn't leave by way of the door."

"Nor did he come in that way, I suspect," Ki said, walking to the window across the room. "See that tree growing outside, and that big branch stretching beside the windowsill? Look how the bark is scuffed on the top of the branch. The knifer probably slid in along it, maybe slipped up on Gothe, or waited till he came in. And I've a notion Gothe got a good look at him before he was stabbed."

"How d'you reckon that?" Beard demanded.

"Take a good look at Gothe's face. Wouldn't you say his expression was one of utter astonishment and disbelief? So big a surprise, in fact, that it left its mark even after death?"

"Sure does, like he was done in by someone he knew well and had no reason to fear," Beard admitted, "and I believe you're right about that branch, too. Say, you don't miss much, do you? You'd make a good deputy sheriff, Ki."

"Take the dealin' job I offered first," Chenault advised Ki. "It'll give you a higher standin' in the community. Dealers have to be intelligent."

"That's right," Beard agreed. "They make barkeeps out of the dumb ones."

Chenault grinned. "I'll have to be getting back downstairs. Can't leave it too long, with all those smart dealers around."

"I'll go tell Doc Terwilliger about this," the sheriff said. "Doc'll be so busy holdin' inquests, he won't have time to pizen anyone for the next week."

Neal Chenault and Sheriff Beard departed together. The clerk dragged the body out onto the room's threadbare throw rug, which did much to break up the bystanders and send them prattling back to their rooms. Jessie and Diedre lingered, but firmly assured by Ki that he was fine, they left as well.

Ki shut the window, and was drawing the blind when there was a knock on the door and Diedre entered. "No, Ki. You cannot stay here, not after all that's happened," she said with a shudder. "Come with me."

"But—"

"Come with me," she insisted, in a tone that brooked no argument.

What the hell, he thought, and obligingly followed as Diedre swished down the hall in her floor-length pegnoir nightgown. Ushered into her room, which was bigger than Gothe's but no better furnished, he asked, "Okay, now what?"

"Now what?" Diedre locked the door, smiling coyly. "Now we go to bed."

Ki regarded the short, narrow bed. "Why, Diedre," he said in mock surprise as she moved closer, "are you suggesting we sleep together?"

"Is that so awful?" she murmured, scrutinizing him with her dark, luminous eyes. Her chin was raised and her uptilted face was yearning. "You saved my life today, and I'm very grateful, personally very grateful."

36

Ki was growing interested, but he was also growing worried about playing her game. He wondered how far she'd tease, how far was *too* far and he didn't care to face any more uproar tonight. "Diedre, you don't have to—"

"I know." She laid her hands on her chest, palms flat, fingers kneading. "I want to."

"I wouldn't mind either, but what about Charlie Wolfe?"

"I'd rather not discuss him. Besides, Charlie isn't here now; you are." She pressed her body against him, her arm circling his back and clinging as she kissed him for a long, burning moment. Ki responded with enthusiasm, kissing her back, feeling her lips clinging hungrily, her breasts mashing against his chest, her hands shifting to rub along his hips.

They broke for air, but she continued to grip intimately, stretching on tiptoe. He untied the ribbon at the throat of her gown and then began to unhook the little clasps of the bodice. "Damn," he growled, fumbling. "The sleepwear some females have . . ."

"You one of them perverts or something?" Diedre laughed a little and opened all the rest of the clasps herself. "Sleepwear's made to be taken off," she added lightly. Shrugging her shoulders, she slipped the gown off and let it blossom around her feet, exposing smooth, unblemished skin, pointed breasts topped by raspberry-sized nipples, and a plump pudendum, with lips accentuated by a thin line of velvety curls.

Aroused, Ki hastened to be rid of his clothes. Diedre stretched out nude on the bed, watching him strip with that vacant, burnt expression some women get when they're ready for sex. She was breathing hard, as though there wasn't enough air in the room, when, naked, Ki lay alongside on the bed and embraced her. His hands moved impulsively, spreading tenderly across her flat stomach and up over her perky breasts. Trembling from

37

his touch, she shuddered and gripped him, pulling him, urging his hand to slide between her legs and along her sleek inner thighs. Her hips slackened, widening to allow him access while she kept murmuring in a low, passionate voice: "Take me, take me, fill me . . ."

But Ki was not ready to take her. He dallied first in the delights of sexual foreplay. He licked the curve of her neck and the tiny lobes of her ears, then lower, nuzzling and kissing one breast at a time. His groin pressed against her pubic bone, and he began pumping his jutting erection along the sensitive crevice between her thighs, yet never quite penetrating her.

Diedre opened and closed her eyes, gasping and whimpering. Her buttocks jerked and quivered, her legs rolling and squirming until they were splayed out on the sheets, one of her feet pushing up against the iron frame of the bed. "Don't tease me, Ki," she mewled, panting harshly. "Put it in, oh, please put it in." In a frenzy, she reached between them and placed his taunting member against the opening of her moist sheath, prodding Ki into herself with her own trembling fingers.

"Now," she sighed breathlessly, seeming to swallow the whole of him up inside her small belly as she arched her back off the small bed. "Now. . ."

Crooning, Diedre kicked her feet out and locked clawing arms and legs firmly around Ki's impaling body. He felt her eager young muscles tightening smoothly around him in a pressuring action of their own, and he set his mind to the delicious ecstasy of the moment. Tighter she wrapped her limbs, deeper she sank her fingernails, rhythmically matching Ki's building tempo as his body pounded hers against the thin mattress.

A squeaky, rickety bunk was not the ideal spot, Ki thought dizzily, for such frantic sport. But that was about all he thought, as they panted in concentration, pummeling each other with ever-quickening strokes. He pumped into her until she was a hot river, until he could feel her not knowing or caring who or what that thing inside her was, just driving up and down inside her with lavish fanaticism.

"Come with me!" she pleaded loudly, as he felt her inner sheath contracting spasmodically from her erupting orgasm—and Ki climaxed with her, spurting deep inside her milking belly. And long after they were both good for nothing, Diedre was still wailing, "Come with me, come!"

"Enough," Ki said. "Whoever's in the adjoining rooms will think I'm beating you."

She calmed down and snuggled against him, damp with sweat, her fingers entwining with his. "Yes, yes I suppose. But Ki, oh, how I wish..."

"Wish."

"There's a madness going on these hills, a madness that's taken my father and Charlie, and's threatening to take my uncle too. I wish I could stop the madness, but I can't. I must do what I can, must make the best of the life I have here...I must make the best of you, Ki.... In a while, again in a while..."

Sighing, she fell asleep.

Ki lay awake beside her, meditating for a time afterwards.

★

Chapter 4

Jessie, aghast at the price, looked from the two bay geldings for hire and snapped, "I see not all the thieves wear guns!"

The toothless old hostler cackled at her outraged expression. "Feed comes high. Everything has to be freighted in. Tell yuh what, lady, it's less if you hire 'em by the week."

"They should live so long," she retorted, though in truth, the horses looked young and healthy. Grudgingly paying the exorbitant charge, she asked, "How do we get to the Whitewash cemetery?"

The hostler jerked convulsively, his sallow face paling. "You—you an' him ain't fixin' to ride out there, are you? Listen, mebbe you two ain't heard, but things go on out there that ain't natural."

"You mean the ghosts, is that it?" Ki asked.

"And worse. Nobody goes out there, nobody in their right mind. The miners and Injuns what's buried there don't cotton to live folk, and I'm a-warning you, prow-

41

lin' about can kill you. Kill you dead as them what's in that bonefield."

"Suppose you let us worry about that," Jessie said. "Now, how do we find the cemetery?"

In a trembly voice, the hostler gave directions. Then he turned and scuttled off toward the rear of the stable, as if Jessie and Ki were already corpses whose presence there was an ill omen.

Leaving, they rode a couple of blocks to the Tarnhauer General Emporium, where Jessie bought saddle-pack supplies, ammunition, and Winchester .44-40 carbines. Ki disliked guns as a rule, but out in desert wilds, a long-range, big-bore firearm was a practical need. His hand weapons were now secreted in the many pockets of his worn leather vest, Ki having changed from his suit into denims, a collarless cotton-twill shirt, and moccasin-style slippers. Jessie too was clad in more workaday clothes this morning, wearing a simple silk blouse and figure-hugging jeans and jacket. A derringer was concealed behind the wide square buckle of her belt, and her custom .38 Colt was holstered at her thigh. This may not have appeared as stylish or feminine as yesterday's outfit, but considering all that had occurred, it was eminently more sensible.

Then, aboard creaky three-quarter rigged saddles, they headed southwest out of Whitewash. Three miles past the town limits, they took a dusty fork which wound southerly. According to the hostler's instructions, this eventually would take them to the valley that contained the suspicious graveyard. They loped along at a leisurely pace to conserve their geldings, finding them to be capable it not very feisty mounts, and after following the trail across a series of crests and sags, they reached the valley about noon. The sun was a white ingot suspended in mid-sky.

The valley was small, its narrow floor and steep, bouldered sides dotted with mesquite and greasewood.

A few copses of cedar or cottonwood also grew along the floor, whose rubbly surface had a slight yet distinct mounded shape, like the crust of a bread loaf. As such it had to be the work of man, not of nature, and resembled the burial grounds of other Indian habitations.

Toward the south end lay the old Whitewash cemetery, several hundred yards square and bordered by rickety wrought-iron fencing. Trees shaded three sides, giving the cemetery at a distance the appearance of a cool oasis. As they neared, though, they found a colder sight in the great granite tomb that bulked at the far corner. It was stark, gray, neo-Grecian in style, with a pitched roof and a Corinthian-pillared facade. The effect was so bleak that the monument seemed to cast a pall of malevolence, of foreboding, over the entire graveyard.

Dismounting, they looped their reins around the bars of the rusty entrance gate, and noticed that just inside, the parched earth was churned raw with numerous hoofprints. Evidently some dozen horses had been passing through the gateway together, coming and going from every part of the cemetery, their branching tracks ending at various grave sites. It conjured the vision of specters rising in dark union from hell, returning thence after nocturnal maraudings astride hoodoo steeds.

Between that nightmare and the malignant image of the vault, Jessie felt a brief chill touch her shoulderblades as she and Ki moved farther into the cemetery. Nothing stirred, nothing sounded, not even a lone bird or insect, yet they kept their senses acutely alert while threading among the marked and unmarked plots. Most of the stakes and crosses hung in pieces of sun-petrified wood; most of the stones were unadorned small tablets, interspersed with ornately chiseled slabs memorializing well-heeled miners who'd died during the gold boom. These were emblazoned with such epitaphs as: *Here Lies Palmer Parker, Kilt Ded in the Crystal Palace over Five Aces;* or *RIP Hoss Prinzoni, Who Expired in Bed at Gilded Lily's Sporting Salon;* and *Easy Ike—A Right Generous Pal with a Nugget.*

They made their way to the far end where, up close, the mausoleum looked even more obdurate and more unearthly than they had first thought. They stepped up to its heavy iron door, which was sealed tight and apparently never opened since the remains of the man who built it were locked within. On the door was a large bronze plaque which read:

JEDEDIAH HARGREAVES
1816–1868
THE RICHEST BLOKE
IN THESE HERE PARTS

Below the inscription was a bas-relief figure of a miner with a pick and a nugget pan, and then the words *No Man Deserves a Finer Berth for Everlasting Sleep.*

Jessie smiled wanly at the obvious esteem in which Jedediah Hargreaves had held himself. She rejoined Ki, and they walked slowly around the blockish shrine, their gaze searching the area for some sign of the ghost raiders.

They totally rejected the notion that these were spooks on a supernatural rampage. Logic, which the superstitious citizenry thereabouts failed to use, told them that even if the spirits of miners and Indians were out a-haunting, they wouldn't need live ammunition or horses to go murder and destroy.

Yet they found nothing. There was no clue that any living humans had been in the area at all recently, save for the hoofprints, which were plainly evident. An answer was here somewhere, they felt sure, yet it seemed as ethereal and elusive as the supposed demons they were seeking.

The report of a rifle shattered the early afternoon silence, and a bullet came out of nowhere to crease Ki's low-crowned hat. He flung himself prone behind a headstone, Jessie diving for another while drawing her pistol, finger curling around the trigger. The discharge echoed through the hills; Jessie thought the shot had been fired from the rocky bank along the south and west of them, and risked peering up to see if she could tell.

The rifle cracked a second time. Chips of granite flew off the edge of the headstone, showering down her back, but now she was sure of the ambusher's location. She glanced across at Ki. "Well?"

"Well, it's to be a stalking game," Ki replied, propped on his elbows. "Whoever's firing will wait us out—or try to."

"Where'd he come from? We've been here for over an hour and haven't noticed a thing. Quiet as it is, we'd surely have heard someone approaching."

Ki shrugged. Regardless of how, the attack was a fact, and neither he nor Jessie had any intention of letting the ambusher get away with it. Jessie voiced their angry resolve when she answered her own query: "Well, we'll just have to head up and ask him."

Cautiously they began working their way toward the slope, darting from stone to stone, keeping as much as possible behind cover. In the silence, the least noise carried. Ki thought he heard a boot scrape rock, and tensed. But it was Jessie who first spied a form as it dipped stealthily out from concealment and started toward a new position.

He never lived to reach it. Jessie's Colt bucked in her fist, and the figure stiffened and sprawled out in the rocks.

Ki then caught a muttered curse that did not come from the man Jessie had shot. "There's another one still hiding up there," he cautioned Jessie in a low, urgent tone. "Stay put and cover me. I'll see if I can't prod him into showing."

Silent and motionless, Jessie waited and watched

while Ki eased slowly to higher ground. The ambusher fired, his bullet answered by two fast slugs from Jessie. Ki vaulted the fence and began dashing up the slope, climbing unconcealed while the ambusher's attention was focused the other way. More shots were traded, and a haze of powder smoke rose from the ambusher's bouldered vantage up the slope and Jessie's poor shelter below. Racing higher, at an angle, Ki approached the spot from above, on the ambusher's blind side, and was almost there when the firing ceased. Perhaps the gunman was reloading, perhaps one of them was hit.

Ki flattened, forcing himself to go slowly and very gently, so as not to be heard now that everything had fallen so quiet again. Again he caught the sound of boots scraping against the rocks. Once more he tensed, listening, realizing the second ambusher was creeping closer, as though moving to a different vantage. The man was definitely trying to act like a snake, slithering and slouching behind rocks; but he was nervous, edgy, not always placing his hard leather boots as quietly as he should.

In such a situation it was understandable for men to grow anxious and twitchy. But Ki grew merely more icy and calculating. He was hunting a vicious sniper, but purposely employed the same cunning and techniques he would use stalking a savage four-legged man-killer. Noiselessly he inched forward, his nimble fingers feeling the razorlike *shuriken* blades that were tucked in his vest pockets. He heard a soft grunt and, aiming for it, listened for more sounds to home in on, until finally he eased into position and stared over, downward.

It was no ghost, real or fake, but a pock-faced man in grubby range duds. He was behind the low rockery of a small ledge, crouching on one knee while sighting a Spencer .56-50 repeater, tensing, prepared to blast Jessie.

Rising, Ki ordered, "Lay it down."

The man pivoted, firing as rapidly as he could lever.

Ki nailed him in the heart and throat.

The ambusher toppled awry with his leg bent under him, his rifle still gripped in one hand, the points of two glittering *shuriken* protruding from his chest and neck. Ki paused, ready to hurl another *shuriken* if need be. A noise behind him made him spin around, but it was only Jessie, scrambling up with her revolver held ready, relief welling in her eyes.

"Thank God," she sighed tremulously. "Is he . . . ?"

"Not yet. But I'm pretty sure he's the last."

Jessie, keeping her revolver trained, walked forward with Ki and stood over the prostrate, dying figure. "Who are you?" she demanded. "Who's your partner? Why'd you try to drygulch us?"

"Don't make no difference now . . ." The man choked, grimacing with pain. "You got him, and I'm slippin' fast. But the boys'll be along . . ."

"So you're in a gang, paradin' as ghosts?"

"Th' devil with you . . ."

"Who's your boss?" she urged. "Who's behind it? You'll feel better if you get it off your conscience."

"Th' devil with me . . ." The man shuddered, his chest heaved once, and he expired, twitching a final faint tattoo on the stony earth.

"Hell!" Disgusted, Jessie turned away.

Ki inspected the dead man's Spencer, but it was a stock '65 Indian model without oddities or markings that might provide clues. Then he and Jessie clambered over the rocks to the first hombre, who was equally a stranger. His rifle was equally standard. From there they scouted for horses, hoping a brand might hold a hint, but couldn't find any trace of them. The men must either have hidden their mounts away or left them with yet a third man. As it was, the best they could conclude was that both men were common gun-thugs, as unwashed and nondescript as their belongings.

Hunting the horses brought Jessie and Ki to a rimrock, from which a scenic panorama of knolls and canyons fell southwestward to the heat-hazy Gila Basin. As they surveyed the view, Jessie observed thoughtfully, "Those gunmen must've been posted to stop anyone snooping around the cemetery. That means something is there, okay, something we've overlooked or failed to recognize. I've no idea what."

"I'm stumped, too, but let's go now before 'the boys' come along."

"It'd be a waste to go back to town, I feel," Jessie asserted on their return to the cemetery. "Ki, do you recall Marshal Ulrich's story I related to you back in Tucson?"

"Sure. The McGeephers got burned out by the ghost raiders, who often rode across their spread between the cemetery and the Basin. If I follow your drift, Jessie, I agree. That route would be worth checking over."

Upon mounting their rented bays, they rode south through the valley and emerged into an open field. Ki began scouting for tracks here, and not surprisingly, he found plenty baked into the gritty soil, interlocking and overlapping every which way. He shifted back a short distance away to survey their general layout, then crisscrossed to sort out and piece together who had gone where with what. Presently he untangled a pattern that seemed to fit. These prints he scrutinized carefully, noting peculiarities in the stride and gait and shoes of various horses. When he was through, he knew he could recognize each set of tracks anywhere now.

The imprints left the field, aiming in the direction of the Basin. For a while they were easily trailed down through the wild fastness of the hills, but at length they descended into a region of knuckled hogbacks, sprouting thatches of briar and bear grass, and stone benches like arid plateaus. There, the prints vanished. Ki had to dismount and lead his gelding as he walked, squinting hard in the glare of the westering sun. Some of his tracking now was done by instinct, once going a half-mile along a gully before he found that his trust had been good. A white scratch, the iron of a horse shoe against a rock . . . and then, a little further on, a stepped-on twig, cracked and showing pulp. But mostly Ki followed logic and experience, a combination of knowing the line of travel taken already and of sensing where it would most likely continue.

There was no sign of pursuit, but Jessie rode cautiously, checking all around—particularly scrutinizing their back trail. They were, after all, following a course traveled by the ghost killer gang, and it could very well be that "the boys" would be along this path. In that regard, she wondered how it could've been any riskier to've stayed up searching the cemetery.

They rode for the better part of the afternoon, until the winding canyons grew shallow and the ridges more rounded, and at last they came to the edge of a gently rolling plateau. The trail Ki had been so diligently unraveling now reappeared clearly in the weedy soil. They traced the prints across the corrugated steppe until suddenly Jessie reined in and pointed to her left.

"The McGeephers ranchhouse, if I don't miss my guess."

"What's left of it," Ki allowed.

Yonder, rubiescent in the lowering sun, were a few charred posts thrusting skyward from an ash-heap foundation, standing watch on a soot-streaked rock hearth and chimney. Off to the side, nearly cut off from view, was the gutted ruin of a barn. The rest of the razed, abandoned McGeephers ranch could've been viewed if they'd angled in that direction, but neither Jessie nor Ki were of a mind to. They had seen enough.

The path continued lengthwise across the deserted tableland, wandering through a succession of interconnecting valleys and canyons. Eventually it cut from the flat into a large arroyo, full of boulders and treacherous underfoot, and soon from there declined through a steep draw, reaching lower and deeper into the broken tailings of the foothills. Trailing became difficult again, but every so often Ki picked up a hoofprint, cigarette stub, or similar clue that proved that they remained on the right track.

Twilight fell softly and quietly as they twisted through eroded culverts and between massive boulders, on a route designed to conceal riders from view. Darkness beat them to the notched draw leading to the Basin floor. From there on stretched a landscape of meager grazeland and occasional farm acreages, of hardy brown grasses and prickly thickets and clumps of bedded livestock, and of rocks—miles upon miles of rocks, lost in the blue heat of dusk.

Still dogging the trail, they let their weary horses set the pace as they crossed the desert plain toward a maze of shallow arroyos. As they drew nearer, Ki noticed on the right, nearby, a craggy outcrop sporting foot-high tufts of bluegrass, an indiction of a spring or tank. He called to Jessie, motioning, and angled toward the boulders. Jessie headed after him. Approaching, the horses quickened, scenting water.

The outcropping encircled a small patch of bottom, where a thin trickle of water oozed from the ground. Dismounting, they loosened saddles and picketed the horses by the meager flow, then knelt in the grass, cupping their hands to drink. Then they ate a cold supper, and were discussing whether to camp there or push on when suddenly Jessie gasped, bolting upright.

"There! See?" she cried, pointing at a flickery crimson glow climbing the western sky a little to the south of them. "A fire! It's got to be!"

"It is. Not grass or brush, not here, and growing awfully big, awfully fast," Ki muttered, peering at the feverish burn swelling up across the angry sky. "Makes me wonder if it had help, like the McGeephers had help."

"Exactly—but in any case, we can't ignore it!"

Ki, already diving for the horses, tightened cinches and checked riggings while Jessie stuffed the saddlebags. Snatching the reins and vaulting into the saddles, they kicked their mounts into stretching runs and kept them heading straight—or as straight as the terrain would allow—while the blaze inflamed the near distance, radiating a fiery beacon.

Across the heat-blasted flats, through mesa-flanking benches and brush-strewn arroyos, they rode low over their geldings' flowing manes, urging them on. Presently, after passing through a straggly belt of tamarack, they came upon a path, thread-thin and rarely used, that wriggled in the same direction. Veering, they followed the path as it skirted a spine of jagged sandstone rises, dog-legged around the last one, and intersected another trail, this one more along the lines of a ranch-wagon road.

They took the road. It too was bearing toward the fire, although like most wagon roads, it took the roundabout easy way and like most ranch roads, it led in turn to each ranch on the way. Yet they made better time, their horses lengthening their strides, the rhythmic beat of their irons quickening, as the hardpan surface unwound among baked stone slabs, through pockets of brush and cactus, and around blind curves of buttes and hummocks.

Verging on yet another blind curve, Jessie and Ki rode without speaking, concerned about their horses' flagging energies. The moon was up, though tonight it had lost some of its previous carmine hue. But now the smoky torch of fire distorted the sky, and the light was filtering through it, eerie and unreal, as they hit the bend. From the other side of the blind curve, a swarm of flickering shadows loomed into view.

Always the wary wolf, Ki still felt his nerves tauten when he glimpsed the mobbing ghouls. They resolved into mounted men, hat brims drawn low, faces muffled in neckerchiefs looped high about their throats. Ki reacted instinctively, jabbing his horse into full gallop as he swept his carbine into firing position. Jessie was a heartbeat behind, moving reflexively; Ki had trained and conditioned her until such responses were automatic. The rest of her mind was working equally swiftly, noting in the first eye-blink that the horsemen were caught unawares. They were riding with loose reins, glancing neither right nor left. But they were well over a dozen strong, and armed to the teeth.

Yet if their numbers were distressing, their features were amazing, if not downright unnerving, and harrowing to boot. The moonlight, reddish and eerie, beat not upon human faces but upon fleshless skulls, grisly death's-heads with cavernous eye sockets, grinning teeth, noseless cavities.

It was a toss-up as to who was more astonished—Ki and Jessie by their prey's diabolical appearance, or the skulls, by the sight of anyone else at all.

The difference was, Jessie and Ki had the initiative.

Ki had triggered, levered, and triggered again before the death's-heads even began to check their mounts. The revolver in Jessie's bucking fist streamed fire and smoke. The air rocked to the echo of thunderous reports, and under the blast of those cycloning guns, the skulls scattered in jostling confusion. Jessie saw one reel back, heard his yell of pain, which was healthily human. A second gave a queer, strangled cough and toppled from his horse, sprawling motionless underhoof on the trail. Others fired erratically in reply, but Jessie and Ki were a flying wedge cannonading broadsides through their midst, and in the frantic melee, they were more apt to hit one another—and did.

A third death's-head gave a howl of pain and rage and pawed madly at his blood-spouting arm. The shock of the heavy slug almost bowled him over, but he kept his saddle, ducking his head, riding away hell-bent for leather. His retreat was the signal for universal panic. Yelling and cursing, the other skulls launched after him, to vanish off amongst the mesquite and greasewood.

Instantly Jessie holstered her smoking Colt, fetched up her carbine, and sent a stream of lead hissing and crackling in pursuit. She had the satisfaction of hearing a wild thrashing and howling, but mainly from the distance ahead came the rattle of hoofs, fast diminishing out of range. She ceased firing, turning to find that Ki had dismounted and was heading for the downed raider. Stepping from her saddle, she hurried to catch up.

"Careful, he may be playing possum," Ki warned as they approached.

But the man was thoroughly dead. Covering his head was a black cloth mask, which had two small slits for eyeholes and was painted with garish white streaks to give the appearance of a grinning skull. Also all-black were his boots, neckerchief, flat hat, leather gloves, and full-length linen duster. Opening the duster, they discovered it was of a reversible style, looking the same either side out—except his on the inside was painted with bone-like designs that, when reversed outside-in and worn with his similarly striped gloves, would make him resemble a ghostly skeletal apparition.

Ripping off his mask and duster revealed an ornery-featured cuss, but who had nothing outstanding or familiar about him. He wore ordinary cotton twill pants and shirt containing only insignificant belongings, and his shell belt and revolver lacked any distinctiveness. But the paint on the mask interested Jessie. She scratched at it with a tentative fingernail, cupping her hand around one of the streaks and gazing at it thoughtfully for a moment—

Until Ki snapped, "C'mon! I think I hear them stirring."

Jessie, straining to listen, caught a whisper scarcely louder than that of sand rippling from the flat. It was sufficient; like Ki, she felt the raiders were liable to regroup fast and charge back after them or their man, or both. So leaving the man where he lay, she quickly folded his black outfit and tucked it in her saddlebags, then remounted, saying to Ki, "Whether they're coming or not, it's time we got on to that fire!"

"Their fire," Ki responded, prodding his horse onward as he loaded his carbine. "They set it, Jessie. I'll bet anything they did."

Chapter 5

For a short stretch Jessie and Ki were flanked by mesquite and chimney rock, as the trail began curving in a gradual sweep toward the mouth of the Blue, at the Gila River. The growth soon thinned to a straggle, then ceased altogether. Riding past the last tangled bush, they came upon open grazeland, which reflected scarlet and ash from the fiery sky.

About a half-mile ahead, on a tree-dappled low rise a few hundred yards off-trail, they saw fenced ranch-grounds enclosing a two-story house, a barn, and other buildings. The barn was a raging blaze, and the ranch-house was burning intensely throughout its whole lower portion with an ember-crackling, smoke-belching roar. Closing fast, they noticed two partly clad men sprawling lifeless by the bunkhouse door and an old duffer in long johns attempting to climb a ladder to the second-floor window at the end of the ranch house. But from a window below gushed increasingly fierce heat and jetting flames, sparking the already smoldering ladder, driving him back each time he tried to mount.

On gut-heaving lathered horses, they reined in by the frantic oldster and dismounted at a run. Jessie called, "Is somebody upstairs?"

"The boss! Both of 'em!" he yammered. "Neither Maddox come down!"

"Maddox!" Ki shot him a probing look. "Diedre Maddox?" Catching his nod, along with his booze-shot eyes and whiskey breath, Ki sized him as a rackabone ex-waddie, fuddle-flustered to a doubt. "Are you sure Diedre's up there?"

"Shore I'm shore! Saw Miz Maddox at her window, till smoke got 'er, an' she fell back afore she could climb out." The oldster pointed at an upper window by the front of the house, then motioned to another window nearer midway. "Ain't seen Mist' Genesee since he went up to bed. But he ain't down here now. Must be up there, too. They're gettin' burned alive!"

Scanning the blazing house, Jessie sighed despairingly. It did seem largely hopeless, Ki had to admit. Downstairs was an inferno, flames erupting and scaling the outer wall almost to the upper windows, and blocking access to either Maddox bedroom. Only by the rear was the fire still below the second story, which was why the oldster had put the ladder at the last window. Ki eyed the ladder speculatively; it promptly burned in two and dropped with a crash. Most of the upper windows were reddened, and back of the open one, Diedre's window, presumably, a funereal glow was beginning to strengthen.

"Fire eating through the floor," Ki reckoned aloud.

"Stairs can't be used. None of the trees are close enough to swing up and in from," Jessie responded glumly. "There's no outside chimney to climb, no verandah roof, no place possible that I can see. Can you?"

"No." Pivoting, he gripped the oldster by the

56

shoulder. "Where can we get rope—sixty feet of good lariat? We'll need a crowbar or a posthole digger, too, or even just a shovel with a strong handle!"

"Ropes are—were—kept in the big barn, but there's a corral shed for spares. The tools are in a shanty o'er thisaway!" At a bandy-legged trot, he led them to the nearby shanty. "Whatcha got in mind?"

"No time now to explain," Ki declared, delving inside.

Jessie felt none too sure she wanted to know. Whatever it turned out to be, his idea was bound to be daredevil risky and, she suspected, so harum-scarum she'd wet her britches worrying.

Ki quickly chose a long-handled spade. Next they hurried to the shed, finding it a snakepit of discarded rope and tack gear. Furiously they dug apart the rope tangle; the lengths were either too short or too rotten or both, until finally Jessie unwound seventy-plus feet of sturdy manila hemp. They hastened outside, Jessie coiling the lariat, Ki eyeing the fire and then turning to the oldster.

"An ax! Can you get me an ax?"

"I knows where there's a hatchet."

"It'll do. Hurry! The fire's climbing fast!"

Obeying, the old puncher stumped for the bunkhouse as fast as his gimpy limbs would permit. Jessie and Ki rushed toward the house, arriving near the back where the ladder had stood. Double-checking, Ki detected no serious flaws in the frayed, worn rope, or any cracks or woodbugs in the seasoned hickory handle of the spade. He noosed the handle in the middle, took a turn and a hitch, and was drawing it tight when the oldster returned, wheezing and stumbling, a broad-bladed hatchet gripped in his gnarled hand.

Thanking him, Ki took the hatchet and thrust its haft in the back of his waistband. He held the spade poised over his shoulder, and stood rigid for a moment, gaug-

57

ing distance and angle. Then his right arm snapped forward. The spade hurtled through the air, leading with its heavy metal head, the rope trailing behind. Right through the second-story window it speared, to land on the floor with a clatter that sounded above the roar of the flames.

"Jehoshaphat—whatta pitch!" the oldster gawked, owl-eyed.

Without commenting, Ki drew the dangling rope taut, whipping the sag up before the flames from the lower window could sear it. As he had figured, the long handle of the spade caught on either side of the window frame and held fast. He dashed to a nearby tree and wound the free end of the rope about its trunk, and with Jessie joining in to pull, drew the length as taut as possible and tied it securely. Then, flashing Jessie a parting grin, Ki gripped the slanting rope and began going up it, hand over hand.

"I knew it," she sighed, returning his smile. "It's a pisser."

The oldster, divining Ki's purpose, yelled a frantic protest. "The rope'll burn through and yuh'll ne'er git down!"

Ki made no reply, saving his breath for the steep climb ahead.

"You'll git caught up there an' roasted, too!" the oldster warned.

Jessie advised, "Save your lungs. Ki doesn't wear ears."

"He do so, I saw 'em!" The oldster gave a snort, then shouted, "They's done suffocated by now, anyway! It's a lost cause, losin' you!"

Now Ki was dangling over the flame-spurting first-floor window. Its furnace breath seared him, and for an instant his senses reeled. Then he gripped the window ledge, drew himself up to a perch, and with his elbow, smashed out the rest of the glass. With a heave and a plunge, he slid through the window frame, past the spade handle, and sprawled on the floor.

Regaining his feet, he crossed the room to the door, feeling its panels for heat before opening it. He peered into a corridor which was dimly lighted by the flames that were coming through the floor. The nearby end door, which doubtless opened onto the rear stairs, was closed. Across the hall was another door, and further along it, a row of four more doors on each side. That matched the number of windows, thank God, making it easier to locate the rooms.

Ki headed up the corridor, counting doors, stopping at Genesee Maddox's room despite his urge to get Diedre. Her uncle needed help as much or more, not having even reached his window.

Finding the door locked, Ki jerked the hatchet from his waistband and began chopping out around the latch plate and striker. Splinters flew, the door's frame and panel splitting and crumbling. Soon he had an opening through to the bedroom, and right then and there he knew he was in for trouble. He could hear flames churning and crackling, and rolling out from the opening was thick smoke and blistering heat. Once he got the door open, a volcano of destruction would pour out of the bedroom. He kept on nevertheless, and after some more cutting, he kicked out the latch assembly and opened the door.

Fire and smoke mushroomed out, and the corridor sprouted incandescence. Ki staggered back, choking, eyes stinging, the smoke-boiling air searing his lungs as he thrust to the doorway again. Squinting in, he saw that over to one side was a tumbled bed, as though someone had risen from it hastily, throwing the covers back in wild confusion. In a corner was a burning chair over which hung burning a pair of breeches, a shirt, and overalls. A burning hat rested on the bedpost. Dangling from the post, under the hat, was a shell-belt. The butt of a revolver protruded from the holster. At the foot of the bed stood a pair of smoking boots. The large middle area of the room had vanished; the floor had collapsed. Fire was blossoming up like a disease through the hole, consuming the bedroom with-avid hunger.

Genesee Maddox was beyond rescue.

Lunging on along the stifling, smoke-reeking corridor, Ki located Diedre Maddox's room near the front stairs. The staircase was gone, and the stairwell groaned from the ominous roar and crackle of the fire rushing up from the furnace below. Her door too was locked. With all his strength, he hacked and hewed, grimly aware that at the other end of the house, more flames were swelling upward, drawing ever closer to his thin manila line of escape.

After what seemed an age, Ki smashed enough to force open the door. The bedroom was more or less intact, missing no great chunks, though the floor was afire in places, and fumes were sifting between the boards. Through the seething murk, he could dimly see Diedre in her peignoir nightgown, a motionless huddle slumped on the floor below the open window.

He started crawling toward her, choking in the supposedly clearer air near the floor. He rose to a crouch and shoved on through the clouding smoke, and after an eternity of blind groping, his hands encountered her limp body. He held her wrist and found the thready beat of her pulse.

"Hang on, you're going to make it," he murmured to the unconscious girl. Whipping out his bandanna, he found her wrists and bound them firmly together. Then he stood up, gasping in the heat, and looped the bound hands about his neck. Diedre was inches shorter and pounds lighter than Ki, but she was no picayune featherweight, either. Carrying her piggyback, Ki stumbled out to the corridor and lurched at a stoop down to the last room, fighting for breath and balance till he gained the broken window.

Shuffling awkwardly, clasping the girl with one arm, Ki maneuvered onto the sill in a sitting position, legs dangling down the wall. Then, grabbing the rope with both hands, he moved off the ledge. Dimly he heard the voice of the old waddie, above the roar of the blaze.

"The rope's scorchin'!" he was bellowing. "She'll part any minute!"

Ki realized their danger. Flames were licking high around, biting crisply at their feet and legs. The rope felt like a red-hot wire, and he could smell it burning. He almost lost his hold and plunged them into the fire when he grasped a spot that was already smouldering.

Hand over hand, he passed out of reach of the flames. The ground was still a long way off, though, and to fall now meant broken bones, or possibly death, for him and his helpless burden. His muscles were trembling, and his arms ached from the strain that threatened to tear his hands free as he continued descending. He was still some twenty feet above the ground when he felt the rope slacken. Down they sailed, Ki still gripping the burned-through rope. He managed to land on his feet, with his knees bent to minimize the shock. It was severe, however, and compounded by Diedre, who dropped like a millstone against him, sledgehammering him flat to the ground.

For a moment everything went black before his eyes. Then he felt the strangling arms of the unconscious girl plucked from around his neck, the heavy drag of her body lifted from his back. Hands propped him upright and someone pressed a dipper of water to his lips. As his head began to clear, Ki recognized the person as Jessie.

"Thank heavens," she said fervently. "Are you okay?"

"Ask me later—like tomorrow," he croaked. Gingerly, he straightened to his feet, still a mite woozy, wincing at the pain when he breathed deeply. After he prodded about his sore chest and checked here and there, he decided some ligaments and tendons might be sprained, but no ribs or bones seemed cracked or broken. Then he and Jessie went over to where Diedre lay on the ground. The oldster was tenderly swabbing her face with a damp rag.

Ki asked, "How is she?"

"Perkin' to." He nodded, grinning. "Yup, awake an' alive any moment—to your credit, I reckon. Me'n Miz Starbuck got to talkin', an' I un'erstand you go by the whittled-down handle o' Ki. Me, I'm Jingo Paloo. Proud to meetcha."

And proud to talk, as Ki soon heard. While ministering to Diedre, the garrulous Jingo Paloo rambled on about his twenty years on the Slash-C—until, moments later, he let out a cheer when Diedre fluttered open her eyes.

After a short spell of coughing and gulping in air, Diedre sat up, head in her hands, looking weak and sounding weaker. "Last I remember is springing for the window in smoke thick enough to've cut with a knife."

Jingo Paloo told of how Ki had gone in and got her, declaring, "That was the gol-durndest slickest shovelwork I e'er seed."

"I dunno," Ki replied, shrugging. "Figured I had to get to the window somehow, and I haven't sprouted wings yet."

Diedre beamed at him. "Nor have I, thanks to you."

"I'm afraid your uncle may've earned his pair. He wasn't in his room. Much of the floor wasn't, either. Clothes were on a chair, boots by the bed, hat and gunbelt on a post. Going by that and the look of the bed, he jumped up and fell through the hole in the floor before he could get dressed."

"He always hung his gun and hat on the bedpost,"

Diedre murmured soberly. "I guess that's what must've happened, Ki. I guess he's gone."

"Everybody gone," Paloo grumbled, staring dazedly at the fire. "Caleb Maddox gettin' done in by wide-loopers last fall—first feller t'be done in by the phantom riders, folks say..."

"That's pure gossip, Jingo. Nobody knows."

"Jus' the same, Miz Maddox, your pa's gone, an' Mist' Genesee always figured 'em for it. T'was account o' them our ol' Chinese chef, Lok Yuan, quit and left day afore yesterday. Shore ain't no question t'was them what torched the house, and drilled pore Henry and Bill when they run outta the bunkhouse half-asleep, to see about the fire. Now Mist' Genesee cashed in, an' the money got cashed out, an' nobody's left but me and them new hands that don't count."

"Money?" Jessie asked. "What money?"

"Twenty thousand dollars, the price Uncle Genesee got for the big herd our crew is driving to the Bar-Z-Bar," Diedre replied. With Paloo's assistance she rose shakily to her feet, and as she straightened her peignoir, she explained: "The Bar-Z-Bar owner, Ephram Zephyr, has a contract to supply the dam construction camp with beef, and he's been buying stock all around at good prices. Uncle collected and brought the money in this afternoon, locking it in the safe in the living room. We were going to take it to the bank tomorrow."

"Only them phantoms musta gotten wind of it somehow. Musta knowed it'd be a boodle, Mist' Genesee havin' just about cleaned out the Slash-C to put that herd t'gether. An' knowed the boys'd all be gone on the drive, havin' got p'raps to the Bar-Z-Bar by now, if they didn't make camp for the night." Paloo's voice had risen to a shrill. "So they come bustin' in here, settin' fire and shootin' down folks. They'd have got me, too, if I hadn't dozed off in the outhouse. By th' time I rousted and got m'self t'gether, them demons had done their damndest—*yeow!*" Paloo shouted, jumping as a crackle of shots sounded inside the burning ranch house.

"Easy, Jingo," Ki said, laying a calming hand on his shoulder. "The fire's got to Genesee's gun on the bedpost. That was the cartridges going off from the heat."

Paloo wiped his damp brow with the back of his hand. "Thought for a minute the phantoms was comin' back to finish us off." He quavered. "It'd be like 'em to do that." He jerked, startled again, as the barn roof collapsed with a deafening crash, then added philosophically, "Wal, one lucky thing. All the hosses the boys didn't use were outta the barn, o'er in the field past the grove."

"And there's plenty of sleeping room in the bunkhouse," Diedre noted, regarding her flame-ravaged home. "As long as the mess hall and cookshack don't catch, we shouldn't run short of food, either. Actually, I've roughed it plenty worse than this, just going out camping with Dad."

Despite her optimistic words, Diedre remained melancholy. She wept a few tears, in fact, as they placed the two murdered crewmen in a shed and covered their half-clothed bodies with blankets. Jingo Paloo took her into the bunkhouse to scrounge up some clothing, while Jessie and Ki tended to their horses, pasturing them with the ranch stock in the field past the grove. By the time they returned, the ranch house as well as the barn were burned down to skeletons of blazing beams and timbers. For a while longer, though, they continued to keep a sharp watch on the roofs of the outbuildings, on the chance that a stray brand might ignite them.

"I imagine that's all for tonight," Diedre announced at length. "We might as well try to catch a little rest."

Jessie nodded. The once blazing flames had burned out, reducing the ranch house and barn to radiant heaps of fuming, guttering coals and embers. "The ashes should be cool by morning. Then we'll see if we can find your uncle's remains for a funeral."

Retiring to the bunkhouse, they bedded down in their clothes. Sleep came slowly but eventually, a welcome respite.

★

Chapter 6

Pale pink dawn was smearing the eastern horizon when
Ki awoke. Careful not to disturb the other sleepers, he
quietly slipped out of the bunkhouse.

The ranch house and barn were blackened ruins, cool
and charred. Probing the ashes and the embers of beams
and timbers would have to wait for better light, Ki reckoned; in the meantime, he scouted the ground about the
yard and points beyond, but found nothing of value.

With sunrise now in full glory, Ki returned to the
bunkhouse. Jessie and Diedre were up, and left for the
cookshack while Ki roused the snoring Jingo Paloo.

"We got an unpleasant chore to do," Ki said, "and it
won't get done with you pounding your bunk."

Yawning, cussing, Paloo groped for his boots. After
a scrounge in the tool shanty, they set to work with
picks and shovels, burrowing into the tangle of blistered
beams and scorched foundations. They had toiled for
perhaps an hour when Paloo suddenly let out a yelp.

"Bones! I see some!"

Ki nodded. "Careful, now, all in through here."

Combing the spot, digging gingerly with shovels, they soon had unearthed a badly burned skeleton. A sickening stench arose from the ashes and caused Paloo to gulp and gag. Last to come to view was the skull of the cremated man. It had become detached from the spinal column, doubtless because of some blow from a falling beam, and lay a foot or two distant from the rest of the pathetic heap. Paloo drew away in horror, but Ki picked up the scorched skull, his interest piqued. He turned it in his hands and studied it thoughtfully.

Then setting it down, Ki asked, "Go get a blanket, will you?"

Paloo took off for the bunkhouse. Ki scrutinized the remainder of the skeleton until Paloo brought the blanket. Then he piled the remains on it and wrapped them up, refraining from asking the shrinking old waddy to assist him. Carrying the bulky bundle away from the ruins, he gently placed it under a tree, then went with Paloo over to the mess hall.

Jessie and Diedre had breakfast about ready. Kitchen domesticity was not a driving passion with Jessie, but she'd felt Diedre could use the company, and wanted to look for sacks or parcel paper in the cookshack. She'd found paper and string, saved by the ex-chef Lok Yuan; and leaving Diedre for a brief while, she'd wrapped the contents of Ki's and her saddlebags.

Now, within minutes of Ki and Paloo's entry, all four of them were partaking of bacon and eggs, flapjacks, and cups of fragrant coffee, appetites unfazed by talk of bones and such-like. They finished with more coffee.

"I suppose," Jessie said, as the meal was ending, "it's easier for folks to attend a burial at Whitewash Cemetery, Diedre. Me, I wouldn't plant a rabid skunk there. But first the law must be told, then likely an inquest held."

"Very well. But I told too much already, y'know,

spreading mean thoughts, those vicious suspicions about Uncle Genesee. I'm so ashamed."

"Don't be, Miz Maddox, plenty feel same's you," Paloo said. "Your uncle was hard to work for, an' never gave no slack. He liked to say crews were like mavericks—they had to be taught who's boss, and be ridden on short rein."

Ki asked in a casual manner: "Was he big enough to do it, Jingo?"

"I hope to shout! Solid and tall, black whiskers and snappin' black eyes, and plumb quick-fisted in enforcin' his own notions about running a spread. 'Tween the drubbin's and his notions, all the old hands who worked for Mist' Caleb have quit, 'cept for me and pore ol' Henry an' Bill. They got too set in the old ways, I grant, but Mist' Genesee brung in some peculiar Brazos ways, too. I mean, it's rummy to practically strip a spread like he did the Slash-C to build that herd. 'Course he earned top price, but he didn't leave much for breeders."

"Brazos?" Jessie asked. "He's Texan?"

"For several years, anyway." Diedre put in. "Sold out a small ranch there when he moved here, I believe. But I don't know just where. I never knew much about him. You see, he wasn't really my uncle. His name wasn't even Maddox, though most people have forgotten about that."

Jessie gasped, taken aback. "Not your uncle?"

"No, only a step-uncle. My grandfather Roland got married a second time, late in life, to a widow with a young son. Their name was Anders, but as the boy grew, he took on my grandfather's name, Maddox. Poor Uncle Genesee! It'd have been better for him to've stayed in Texas, the way things worked out."

On that disheartening note, they left the table. Ki returned to the ruins and shifted beams and timber until he had uncovered a ponderous iron safe that stood in what had been the living room. The door stood open, and the inner compartment had been smashed. He examined the combination knob and tumblers carefully, his brows drawing together in thought, an inscrutable expression in his onyx eyes. He was just straightening from the safe when a clatter of hoofs sounded and a rider bulged out of the trees to the northeast. He was a young fellow in cowhand garb, his eyes wild, his face haggard. His hatless head was wrapped in a bloody rag.

"The herd!" he yelled as he flung himself from his reeling saddle. "Rustled in Bleaker Canyon! Coupla the boys cashed in! Others rode t'town t'get the sheriff, and I come t'tell the boss! Hell's bells, what's been goin' on here?"

Paloo told him, toning down considerably as Jessie and Diedre hurried up within earshot. The cowhand stared dazedly about, and raised a shaking hand to his bloody face. Jessie took him by one arm, Diedre by the other, and they gently led him toward the bunkhouse.

"Come on and lie down. I'll take a look at that head," Jessie said, and Diedre called over her shoulder, "Jingo, get the salve and the roll of bandages in the shed behind the tool-shanty. We'll need hot water and cloths, too."

While Paloo was gone and Ki was after water and cloths in the cookshack, Jessie removed the blood-soaked rag and examined the puncher's wound. It proved to be a ragged furrow at the hairline above his left temple. Paloo and Ki came in about then, but she ignored them while she concentrated on probing the skullbone with sensitive fingers.

"Just creased—nothing broken," she stated. "I'll wash and tie it up."

With deft fingers she cared for the wound. Paloo brought in hot coffee, and after a cup and a cigarette, the young puncher recovered his composure somewhat.

"We never had a chance," he replied to their questioning. "It was just before dawn, all gray and no light, when them demons shot the two nighthawks and shot us up in camp. Then they stampeded the herd from the canyon. By the time we got ourselves patched and riding, they was plumb out of sight and hearin'. We follered 'em, but lost their trail after a spell. Decided we better hightail back for help. Reckon the herd's halfway to Mexico by now."

"If I understand right," Diedre said, rather anxiously, "you hadn't delivered the herd to the Bar-Z-Bar when it was rustled?"

The puncher nodded. "The boss told us not to run the fat off them critters, so we bedded down in Bleaker Canyon, figuring to ease in to the Bar-Z-Bar t'day. Maddox rode on ahead and collected the pay from Zephyr."

Diedre paled. "Oh, no!"

"Yes'm, I believe he did. Told our foreman he wanted to get to town and the bank with it before dark. You could check direct with Gillespie about that, I reckon, 'cept he's one of the dead 'uns. And Ephram Zephyr already looked the herd over and was pretty well satisfied with his bargain, so he may've paid, okay."

"No doubt. We and the Zephyrs have been neighbors for years, and I'm sure Ephram figured it'd be fine," Diedre allowed glumly. "But his paying in advance doesn't make it a sale, not till we deliver. And Uncle Genesee put the money into our safe here last night. He didn't ride to the bank at all."

"P'raps he might've been held up, and figured he couldn't get there before closin' time," the puncher suggested. "Say, you figure we got hit by the same outfit that burned you out and stole the money?"

Ki spoke up. "How far to Bleaker Canyon?"

"About twenty miles," Paloo said.

"Well, it was quite a bit before midnight when they hit here. They would've had plenty of time to get there

71

and pull the wide-looping just before daybreak," Ki responded, answering the puncher's question. Then he asked another of his own: "Did you get a good look at any of the rustlers?"

"Nope," the puncher replied. "They was all over us before we knowed what happened. But I'd be willin' to swear they had skullbones for faces, and that big, tall goblin on a black hoss was headin' 'em, same as usual!"

Diedre glanced sharply at the puncher, but refrained from comment. Jessie caught her glance, and then stared curiously at the young puncher. His hands were shaking and his face was beaded with sweat. He undoubtedly believed that he had looked upon some inhuman monstrosity.

"I think it's about time we ride to Whitewash and notify the sheriff's office what's happened here," Jessie advised Diedre. "This fellow can stay here and look after things till someone shows up."

"Look after what?" the puncher asked. "No house, barn, no stock . . . what's there left to lose?"

"The Slash-C," Diedre answered, turning to leave.

After loading Genesee's bones and the bodies of Henry and Bill onto packhorses, they set off for Whitewash. As they rode the long, dusty miles, the morning grew to a scorching day, clear and cloudless. The sun was an ingot well up in the sky when they reined in at the town's law office and went inside.

An elderly deputy was in charge. Introduced to Jessie and Ki, he gave his name as Web Nudelman, then informed Diedre, "Sheriff Beard rode to Bleaker Canyon a few hours ago, with your hands and a small posse. What can I do for you?"

Diedre and Paloo recounted the tragic events.

"Dunno what this country's comin' to," Nudelman declared querulously. "C'mon, let's go to Doc Terwilliger, him bein' the local coronor."

As they were leaving the law office, Diedre asked

Nudelman, "Will this take long? I really must get to talking with Mr. Hevis at the bank, and Ephram Zephyr. The Slash-C not only lost the herd, y'see, but will have to make good the advance pay, seeing as it was stolen while in Uncle Genesee's care."

"Go ahead, Miss Maddox. We won't need yuh t' help drop off the dead, and Jingo and these folks can tell the doc what's what."

Thanking him, Diedre hastened uptown toward the Southeastern Cattleman's Exchange and Trust Bank. Deputy Nudelman and the others headed down the street, walking their mounts and pack-horses to the doctor's home clinic.

Approaching Terwilliger's house, they saw Charlie Wolfe coming outside, coatless, left shirt-sleeve rolled up and his forearm bandaged. He gave them an acknowledging nod as he started across the street to a horse-lined hitchrail. Nudelman grunted, watching hard-eyed while Wolfe somewhat clumsily unhitched a splendid black stallion, mounted, and then rode on down the street. With another grunt, the deputy led the way along the side of the clinic to a tiepost and entrance marked *Private*. Paunchy Doc Terwilliger looked up from a table as they came in.

"Howdy, Doc," Nudelman greeted him. "What's the trouble with Charlie Wolfe? Saw he had his arm in windings."

"Bullet graze—just a flesh wound," Terwilliger replied. "Said he was ridin' home last night and somebody pitched lead at him out of the dark."

"I reckon there's several somebodies who'd like to do that," Nudelman growled. "Howmsoever, these cit'zens got deliveries to report."

Doc Terwilliger listened without comment. After they finished their story and carried in their gruesome cargo, he said, "Beard should be back soon with the Slash-C punchers that were killed this morning. Assumin' there's time, I'll sit this afternoon on the whole batch and that dealer, Gothe. Sure's a hard loss for Miss Maddox—no ma, her pa goin', now her uncle, too."

"Maybe Lucian Hevis is sweet on her 'nuff to fix that. She needs a good man to side her, and keep that dratted Wolfe from hangin' round," Nudelman commented.

"You're sure down on Wolfe, aren't you?" Ki asked the deputy.

"Ain't my place to pass judgement, Mist' Ki, but I can pass what folks are opinin'. Among other things, they say them devil raiders are led by a big 'un on a horse black as Satan. Did yuh happen to lamp what Wolfe was ridin'?"

Jessie protested, "Why, many honest people ride black horses."

"Now, Nudelman isn't accusin' the boy," Doc Terwilliger said. "But just the same, the ghost business picked up a couple months back, right after Wolfe got out of jail for brand-blotting and cow-stealing from the Slash-C . . ."

Jessie mulled over this interesting point as they departed the clinic a short time later. Nudelman went back to the law office while Jessie, Ki, and Paloo brought the horses to the livery, stabling the Slash-C–branded ones, and turning in the hired mounts and gear. Emptying their saddlebags, Jessie and Ki took her paper-wrapped bundles and strode to the Rosebud with Paloo. He angled for the bar; they headed for their rooms. The desk clerk gave Ki new accommodations, next door to Jessie.

Stashing the parcels in Jessie's room, they freshened up and left to go out again. They were dropping off their keys at the desk when the owner, Neal Chenault, came over. Greeting them cordially, he motioned toward the barroom, where they could see Paloo rambling tipsily among the patrons.

"Jingo's been regaling us with what you did at the Slash-C," Chenault remarked to Ki. "Not many would take such a risk, and it showed mighty fast thinking, too. Is he right? You found Genesee Maddox's cremated bones in the ashes?"

"Yeah, we found bones," Ki admitted.

"Poor sinner. Maddox wasn't in much, but he always handled his drinking and gambling real decent—played poker nifty as most dealers. I told him so, even offered him a job." Chuckling, Chenault then turned to Jessie. "Speaking of offers, may I offer you supper this evening?"

"Aren't you rather impulsive," Jessie teased, "inviting me to dine on such short aquaintance?"

"Think fast, act fast. Shall we say at eight?"

"I hate to think how you'd act if I say no. We shall."

Chenault grinned. "Till then, Miss Starbuck. G'bye, Ki."

For a moment Jessie watched Chenault go on about his business, then walked across the lobby to the entrance, pertly telling Ki, "And you can just wipe that cheesy smirk off your face."

They started for the telegraph office, but then Sheriff Beard and his posse rode into town. He didn't bring any rustlers with him, but did have four horse-draped bodies of punchers along, and was accompanied by the rest of the Slash-C outfit. As the riders reined in at Doc Terwilliger's, Jessie returned to the hotel, while Jingo Paloo tore reeling outside to meet them. The Slash-C crew proved to be likeable sorts, full of piss and vinegar, arriving mad as boiled hornets. They received Paloo's story with lurid profanity.

"The spread's sure gotten tromped," one hand complained to Ki, as they moved the bodies into the clinic. "Don't know how it'll affect us. We may be out of jobs."

A bull-bodied puncher snarled in response, "Who

75

much cares? I un'erstand the new owner's a young filly fresh from school-halterin'."

"You haven't met Miss Maddox?" Ki asked.

"Nope. Hell, we're just gettin' to know each other. Ain't been t'gether but a month or so. Mist' Genesee pulled us from different spreads far 'round, promisin' good wages, and I reckon we can scatter right back to 'em."

The crew soon broke for the Rosebud to drown their grievances. By then Jessie had rejoined Ki, and catching Doc and the sheriff alone in the clinic, they related their galloping clash with the raiders. As they spoke, Jessie unwrapped two parcels that she'd fetched from her room, revealing the dead raider's hood, gloves, and duster.

Beard gawped. "Well, I'll be! So that's how it's done!"

"Plain to see now!" Terwilliger growled. "They appear or disappear by whippin' the mask and mitts on or off, and switcheroo-ing the duster."

"In the same way," Ki said, "their horses could be painted too, and rigged with a cover like a dark sheet that could be raised or lowered."

"Wal, their spookin' won't scarify no more, now that we got this costume to show it's pure flimflam," the sheriff asserted. "Be a sore loss for 'em, but watch out —they're sore losers."

"Problem is, nobody knows who to watch out for. That's why we took care to get these duds to you directly, privately," Jessie explained. "Everyone in the gang is concealed, and disguised to boot. It's the sort of stunt pulled by outlaws who're known around their area, maybe seeming to lead decent, even respectable, lives."

Ki nodded. "Fits. The dead gunman was gone."

"Whaddyuh mean, *gone?*"

"Easy, Sheriff, I didn't up and wander. When I scouted at dawn, there was fresh sign, indicating his pals took his body, no doubt so we couldn't find out who he was, and by association, figure out who they probably are."

Terwilliger said, "Sounds sensible. It all has, more'n what I've heard in the past year. Y'all done a grand turn, and the community owes you a vote of gratitude." He lowered his voice. "I trust not posthumously. . ."

Leaving the clinic, Jessie and Ki again headed for the telegraph office adjoining the depot. There Jessie wired a long, encoded message to the Circle Star Ranch, requesting information about sundry names and data they'd chanced across on the trip so far. Replies were needed as soon as possible, sent care of the Rosebud Hotel.

After paying the telegrapher, they hunted for a restaurant. The day was lengthening into late afternoon—the dull stretch before the flurry of evening trade. The occasional local farmer or rancher moseyed by on horseback or in wagons, and on the boardwalks, a few bonneted women shopped, while bored storekeepers leaned in the open doorways. The bulk of dam laborers was not yet off work; those who were were rooted in the cooler dimness of saloons.

The Eats Café was more akin to a parlor, with a worn Oriental carpet, and a large red-based lantern suspended by gold chains from the ceiling. A blowsy waitress was leaning on the bottom half of the kitchen dutch-door, arguing with an unseen chef, who liked banging pots and pans. There weren't many customers, so Jessie and Ki were able to select a table at the front window. They ordered the blue-plate special on the advice of the waitress: "It'll fill your tapeworm."

The food proved better than expected. They were about halfway through when Diedre Maddox walked by the window, saw them, and came in to join their table. She looked a bit frazzled, and no wonder, having just

77

finished meeting with Ephram Zephyr and Lucian Hevis at the bank.

"The Slash-C is broke," she stated, coming directly to the point. "Broke and in debt. Eph Zephyr agreed to take installments, despite his own squeeze for money, and I gave him a note for twenty thousand, secured by the ranch. As long as I meet the installments, he won't foreclose. He wants to help, and was quite generous, canceling his contract with my uncle—the agreement to supply him regular cattle shipments, which he needs to fill his own contract with the dam construction camp."

Jessie glanced up sharply. "Cancel how? Withdrawn, or voided?"

"He said nullified."

"Yes, null and void. What good news! Now you can sell direct to the construction camp and earn more profit."

"I doubt they'd buy from me, Jessie. As I understand it, they deal only with large, steady shippers."

Jessie smiled slightly. "I've a hunch they'll deal with you. There's one or two chaps I know in that line, who'll surely agree to lend a hand."

"Even assuming they deal, I may not have any stock to sell," Diedre protested. "Paloo says the spread was virtually stripped to gather that last herd."

"I never yet saw a spread," Ki declared jauntily, "where a resolute crew couldn't chouse a hefty passel of fat beefs from the brakes and canyons. I'd bet you'll find that's the condition on the Slash-C."

"I hope. The crew can try, anyhow, for as long as I'm able to pay. I've some money, not a great deal, left me by my grandmother. Apart from the ranch." Diedre gave Ki, then Jessie, a speculative look. "The foreman, Gillespie, died this morning, as you know, and I badly need a *segundo* to take charge," she told them. "Will you take the job, Ki? Can he, Jessie?"

Jessie laughed. "I'm not his boss. But believe me,

Ki's bored by the dam ceremony fanfare, and you'd help us both by taking him from underfoot."

Ki considered a moment longer, gazing thoughtfully out the cafe window. Of course Jessie was correct, but beyond that, he had a feeling that the Slash-C was going to be a focal point of activity.

"Okay, Diedre, I'll make a stab at it."

"Wonderful! When you finish here, we better see about our crew. They may've all quit, y'know; many hands don't cotton to working for a woman boss."

"Every man does, sometime or other," Ki observed.

Soon after, when Ki and Diedre were entering the Rose-bud, they noticed it was beginning to draw a crowd, though the evening was still too early for heavy action. Just in case of a scuffle, Ki had a brief word with Neal Chenault, who assured Ki he didn't care; he could tally the damages faster than anyone could bust up the joint.

Diedre looked perturbed by the talk, but said nothing as they moved on until they neared the barroom. "Ki, ladies aren't supposed to go in there."

"You're not a lady. You're a ranch owner, going after your crew."

They went on into the barroom, then, looking for the Slash-C crewmen. Ki spotted several knots of quiet, watchful gents who kept to themselves, drank without undue show of emotion, and kept a watch on happenings around them. Almost to a man they wore common range-rider garb, faded and frayed, bristling with weapons. The bar counter and tables mostly hosted non-descript ranch hands and construction laborers, who gravitated in groups of friends and co-workers, oblivious to their surroundings. The Slash-C crew comprised just such a bunch at the bar and close-by tables. Escorting Diedre toward them, Ki could hear the dull roar of talking and laughing, the clink of glasses and bottles, then the hurrawin' welcome of a soused Jingo Paloo.

Punchers turned, ready to give Ki a boisterous greeting—then choked, gawking at the tasty young morsel accompanying him. Only Paloo among them knew her identity, but after he whooped out her name, they all knew who she was . . . what she was. The last of their banter drifted low, until a leery hush fell, eyes glaring at the two strangers in their midst.

Ki scanned the crew, catching the few he'd met previously, tagging the most likely troublemakers—who inevitably were the hugest brutes; it never failed. And all, he felt sure, must be silently wishing Diedre would go away, while she must be wishing she *could* go away. But the girl had grit; she stood solid, introducing herself and Ki with a spit-in-the-eye defiance. Then she immediately issued her first orders.

"Drink hearty, fellows," she began. "Tomorrow on you're combing strays out of the broken sections and canyons on the north range—"

A cynical chortling cut her short, the puncher scornful. "Aw, hell, don't pay her no mind, boys." He was the burly pug Ki had spoken to earlier outside the clinic. "Y'know how females go on the prod."

And Ki felt a tiny something go snap inside, like a watch-spring wound too tight. His voice was as steel-cold as his eyes. "Who made you foreman to tell 'em what to do?"

"Eh, nobody, but I can say wha—"

"What's your name? Anyone give you a name?"

"Wha—? Eh, Everts, Paul Everts, but you—"

"I'm foreman, Everts. Long as you draw Slash-C pay, I'm your foreman. Miss Maddox warned me she had problems, and now I can sure understand why, with a slob like you fake-roddin' this litter of snot-nosed lazy whelps."

The others were gaping, dumbfounded, but Everts was growing crimson, champing at the bit. "Enough, squinty, don't press your luck."

"It's not luck. It's the way it is, and if you can't catch on, that's your hard luck." Surveying the others, Ki added, "Dry your ears, listen up. Genesee Maddox wasn't the boss. He worked for Miss Maddox, same's you always have. But whoever's boss, you were hired to side the Slash-C. That makes you beholden' however you reckon, with no excuse for turning traitor to your ranch. So ratters get out. But if you've any pride in yourself, your job, your ranch, you're going to put your brains and guts and, by God, loyalty to the struggle."

"Hell, the cowdung's flyin' too fast for me," another puncher sneered. "And I say *dung* only 'cause a lady's here. 'Cept ladies wouldn't come here."

A third waddie stiffened. "Watch your clapper, Vaughn."

And a fourth: "Yeah, ain't no call—"

"Shuddup, Hudson," the man called Vaughn snarled. "Maybe your spine is made outta smoke, but for me, I had my fill of wimmin's orders as a kid." He got up from his table, a dark, squat man with a barrel chest and black, beady eyes. Without a word, Paul Everts and a third beefy puncher from the bar shoved through to join him. They began wedging their way out of the tight clump of crewmen. "If I craved naggin', I'd get married," Vaughn was scoffing. Then, bumping against Paloo, he growled, "Step aside, lest I squash yuh."

Booze-foolish, Paloo put a hand lightly on Vaughn's arm. "Shimmer dow', hear 'im out. Maybe—"

"Leggo!" Vaughn wrenched away as though rubbed by a snake, then pivoted and gripped Paloo by the shirt, drawing back a ponderous fist to punch the old waddie in the face. The next instant he yelled with agony as slim, bronzed fingers like rods of nickel steel closed on his wrist in a grip that ground the bones together.

"Lay off," Ki said evenly, releasing the wrist. "It was harmless, and Jingo's twice your age and half your weight."

81

"But you ain't, highpockets!" Vaughn bellowed, and let drive at Ki.

With a thin, quirked grin that masked his anger, Ki ducked Vaughn's fist, catching the puncher's outflung arm and angling to drop to one knee, swinging him into *seoi otoshi,* the kneeling shoulder throw. Vaughn arched through the air, over the heads of those at the adjoining table, and came down on the free lunch counter just beyond, atop a sandwich platter and a tray of deviled eggs. He sprawled there, dazed and breathless.

Even before Vaughn hit, Ki was hustling Diedre out of danger's way, deaf to her shrill insistence that they quit, that they leave. Thrusting her through the cramped circle of crewmen, he pivoted to check whatever Everts and his buddies might be up to. Everts was charging with outstretched arms, as if he were tackling a drunk in an open brawl. Ki chopped the edge of his hand down on Evert's nose, tempering his blow so as not to break the nose, but forcefully enough to hurt like howling blazes. Everts screamed, tears of pain springing into his eyes. Ki followed through by kicking him in the side of the knee, collapsing one side. He caught Everts right arm, crunched down on it with his elbow, and then brought his own knee into his hip.

Everts dropped to the floor, leaving the way clear for the third man to lash out at Ki with his wide leather belt. Ki had already seen him slide off his belt and fold it double; he had been keeping track of it peripherally until ready to deal with it. Now, stepping over Vaughn, Ki caught hold of the other man's right arm and left shoulder with his hands. Simultaneously, he moved his right foot slightly in back of the man, so that as the man began tumbling sideways, Ki was able to dip to his right knee and yank viciously. His *hizi otoshi,* or elbow drop, worked perfectly; the man sailed upside-down and collapsed jarringly on top of Everts, flattening them both to the floor.

Vaughn, face purpling with rage, dove swinging at Ki. He'd launched himself off the table while Ki was facing the man with the belt, surging in to where he was almost behind Ki, then lashing out to catch Ki unaware. He very nearly succeeded, but for Ki's glimpsing his move at the last instant.

A roundhouse haymaker swung, grazing against Ki's jaw before he could fully swerve aside. The blow's meaty impact sent him staggering. Wincing with pain, Ki shook his head to clear it, falling back to regain his footing.

"Stand clear, boys, give him room to hit the dirt!" Vaughn called, contemptuous and confident. "Any o' you guys know I just hafta tap once to snuff a galoot's lamp out."

It was then Ki struck back with a jolting uppercut. As skilled in unarmed combat as Ki was, he could've maimed or killed Vaughn easily, and a part of him was provoked enough to do so. But that might've soured relations with the other crewmen, eroding his authority as foreman. Besides, he was furious at the rude, shabby treatment accorded Diedre, and he couldn't think of a better venting than to beat this lout at his own game, the crude brawl.

Ki followed the uppercut with a one-two combination, his punch starting from his shoulder, smashing in like a club. Vaughn tried to jerk backward to evade the blow, but Ki had stomped his right foot atop Vaughn's left boot, momentarily nailing the boot in place. In that moment, Vaughn lurched, tilting off-guard and into range, and Ki kissed five knuckles square in his nose, turning Vaughn's face into a blob of red and driving him almost to his knees. While Vaughn was in that squatting position, Ki's left fist hammered into his chest and hurled him, squalling, back into the clustered crewmen, where he lay still.

Now Ki turned slightly as, with a yell, Everts

pounced at him, and some of the punchers joined in. A backward wing of Ki's arm caught Everts in the throat, flipping him ass over bootheels into a front window, which shattered in a cascade of glass shards. Everts jack-knifed outside, bowling into a trio of loafers and a pet dog napping on a plank bench. The bench upended, splintering in half, catapulting the loafers away, while evidently by the tumult below the window ledge, the mutt was churlishly biting Everts.

Another crewman made a wild grab for Ki. Pivoting aside, Ki snagged him by his belt and neck and heaved him sliding down the length of the bar counter. The customers hastily snatched their drinks out of his path along the counter. The man plunged off into a wet mop and a bucket of dirty water, which the swamper had negligently left there after swabbing the back-bar floor.

By now the barroom was a mob scene, the portion manned by the Slash-C crew in a state of seige. Throngs crushed around, faces pressed to window panes, while men and women converged from within the hotel and out along the street. Ki ducked a straight-arm knuckler, one of his own fists connecting with another puncher's face, dropping the man like a sack of potatoes. Glancing around, he caught sight of Diedre and Paloo safe on the sidelines. Then, weaving aside, he jammed the heel of his right hand into yet another man's face. The crewman blundered against a stack of metal trays, toppling with them with a stunning clatter. Swiveling to spot his next challenger, Ki flicked an antagonistic glance at the horde ringing him. They could've stopped it if they'd cared to, if they'd the courage to step in, he thought irritably. Then he almost had to laugh, glimpsing Neal Chenault—true to his word, placidly marking score on a big yellow notepad.

A chair whizzed past Ki's head, striking the back-bar mirror and cracking it. One tempestuous waddie charged in, swinging a table-leg. He only came partway, as Ki, springing the short distance with a leaping kick, caught him in the solar plexus. The puncher careened back to slam against the bar, his makeshift truncheon flying. But it was befitting, all in all, that his last opponent should be Vaughn, revived and spurred on by a couple of jokers. He vaulted onto Ki's back, encircling his throat with one arm and trying for a strangle hold. That arm was taken in an implacable grip, pulled straight out. Bending slightly, Ki hurled Vaughn through the air against the two goading punchers. The two collapsed, legs unhinged, and fell heavily in a heap.

"Gawd, he downed Vaughn quick ag'in!" a puncher declared in awe.

Ki heard another say, "All three're still seein' twinklies!"

"He tuckered the cream o' our bunkhouse," Hudson allowed, then guffawed. "By Christ, Lennie will stink of that mop-bucket bath for the next month!"

Without comment Ki brushed himself off and motioned for the crew to gather around. They congregated silently, some chagrined, some gaping, a few moaning or limping, but saying nothing.

Ki waited till Diedre was alongside, then broke the silence. "You worked for this woman all along. Guess you didn't know it, but you don't seem to've suffered —just softened. Now you know, so make up your minds. Quit or stay."

Surprisingly, it was Everts who first spoke up, waggling a loose tooth. "Wal, boys, I reckon Miss Maddox might have something. She sure's got a powerful persuader, that's kinda got me convinced."

"Okay, count me in."

"Me, too. I ain't no crawfish."

"We gotta, else we'll end up grub-linin'."

A concensus of agreement swelled from the crew—except for Vaughn, who quit and staggered off after he came to. The Slash-C hands grouped about Diedre, hats

85

in hands, awkward and diffident at first, but she soon put them at their ease. After she had talked with each in turn, Ki had his say:

"Whoop it up as high as you want to tonight, but I want every one of you work-dodgers on the job in the morning. I want every saleable beef flushed out of those brakes and canyons. We'd ought to get a good herd together by the end of the week."

"We'll get 'em," his men declared. "Anything you say, boss."

Chapter 7

The sun blazed lower, burning down the day. By seven, the molten fireball sat rimming the horizon, continuing its slow decline into evening, its slanting rays burnishing the western exposure of Whitewash.

On her way to the Rosebud, Jessie was forced to crimp her hatbrim and squint as fiery glare pierced across roof ridges, casting askance on buildings, and flashing off their windows. The street below was tinged bluish by lengthening shadows, she noticed while crossing, though the roadbed still radiated a torpid heat, made suffocating by dust-churning activity. The town was livening up now with the approach of dusk. Night-bloomers were cropping up among the influx of plain folk doing business—lofty ceremonial delegates, and dam laborers who'd come off work, footloose and fancyin' a spree.

Scanning the ebb and flow around her, Jessie kept an eye peeled for delegates. Since their return a few hours ago from touring the dam site, a few at a time had drawn her aside, chiding her for shirking her dam duties. Or they had come one at a time, hinting a stiff romp would cure her ills. Antagonized by both counts fit to box their ears, she managed to remain civil whenever collared. But it was over the fight in the Rosebud bar that she nigh blew her temper. Some delegates had blamed her for bringing scandal by bringing Ki, accusing her of employing a hooligan as a servant.

She'd lost her temper then, Jessie recalled as she entered the hotel; and she would've blown, if the sheriff hadn't interrupted to announce the inquest was convening. The doc held it with brevity, guiding his coroner's jury of shanghaied bar patrons through the cases of gambler Emile Gothe, the Slash-C punchers, and the blanket of charred bones. Jessie and Ki testified, as did others including Diedre, Chenault—and the sheriff, who produced the ghost raider's costume as evidence, to the shocked consternation of the jury and spectators. At last the jury deliberated, and its verdict was short and laconic, and typical of the cow country:

"Genesee Maddox is the bones. Him and the others listed below came to their deaths at the hands of parties unknown, who have a hanging coming. We recommend the sheriff brings in more spook-suit wearers pronto."

Sheriff Beard gave an indignant yelp when the verdict was read, and subsided to choleric splutters as the inquest adjourned. Afterwards Ki and Diedre briefed Jessie on the fight, which Diedre insisted was by the Slash-C, of the Slash-C—and for the Slash-C to pay amends.

Jessie had some doubts. She hadn't seen the barroom yet, but going by the tales of ravaged shambles, she reckoned the damages could run steep. That was a cost of living on the frontier, where men were judged by their brawn. It was the price, however high, that it took for Ki to win over the crew. They seemed eager to work their tails off now—and they'd have to, and then some, before Ki or anyone else could revive the ranch. When it got waxing fat, Diedre could choose to settle the damages, Jessie thought, but until then . . .

"Diedre," she advised cryptically, "take the costs out of Ki's wages."

Now, as she continued reviewing the afternoon's events, Jessie went upstairs to her room. They had a puzzle, she and Ki. They'd chanced across some of the pieces, and had scattered bait to see what else might develop, and now she wanted to sort out what they had, and get some notion of which pieces were still missing. There was still almost an hour before her supper engagement with Neal Chenault, but there were a number of other things she wanted to, including watch the maids iron her dressy suit. But mainly she thought.

At eight, Jessie sashayed down to the lobby, looking for Chenault. She found a great many others; the lobby was aswarm with a mingle of ages and types, as were the dining salon and the barroom. Still scouting for Chenault, and curious to survey the fight scene, Jessie was crossing into the barroom when Chenault loomed out of the crowd ahead. He wasn't ready for their engagement, Jessie surmised; at least, he better not be. He still was wearing his cutaway business suit, white shirt and black string tie, all showing slight wrinkles and other minor signs of a day's hard usage. Nor was he through with work yet, to judge by the large canvas money-sack he was holding.

"Jessie, you appear ravishing and smack on time," he affably greeted her. "Far superior to your host, I'm afraid. I'm running late."

"But fast, Mr. Chenault. We're to first names in one fell swoop, are we?" she bantered, smiling, shifting to eye the barroom.

"Best not, Jessie. We've cleared away a lot, but still . . ."

Confidently she said, "I've seen my share of havoc,

89

Neal, and probably worse," and she gazed about the room, assessing what was there, deducing what was gone, figuring in the cleanup. "I retract that, Neal," she said, marveling at the destruction. "I'll cable for funds tonight, so you can begin restoring without delay—"

"No, Jessie, thanks. It's not your debt, or Ki's. I asked for it. The train robbery gloomed your usual payday fling, customers moping, nursing drinks, pockets dry as throats. They craved a diversion, so I gave Ki the go-ahead, even boasted he couldn't wreck faster than I'd tally. Underestimated him, there." Chenault chuckled. "Well, they got roused. Money's scarce, but 'tween them and all the rubbernecks coming in to ogle, we're drawing a busy trade tonight. Why, that fight was a favor, and lucky, too. Wasn't yet five when a new dealer walked in, asking for a job"—Chenault gestured at the main poker table nearby. "I hired him to replace Gothe, soon's he showed me what he could do with cards. Listen, I'm through after I do this collection. Don't budge."

Jessie watched Chenault wend back to the bar, then move behind it, emptying his money tills into his sack. Shifting her gaze to the room in general, her roving eye quickly focused on the new dealer.

Presiding over a six-player game, the man was tall, broad-shouldered, clad in the conventional black garb of a gambler. His motions were casual yet deft, his hands slender, muscular, with tapering fingers. Blond-haired, he had a rather pale face, save for a darkening at his cheek-bones and around his deep-set black eyes, with a long, jagged scar extending from the left corner of his mouth almost to the cheekbone.

When Chenault returned, sack full, Jessie remarked, "Handsome man, save for that bad knife scar. Where's he hail from?"

"Y'mean Osmond, the dealer? Well, he didn't say, and I didn't ask." Chenault lapsed into silence as he shouldered through the crowd, leading Jessie back to the lobby. Arear of the reception desk was a short hallway connecting to a rear exit, with a door along each side. Chenault ushered Jessie through the right-hand door, lighting a tablelamp and saying, "No, all I know about him is he rode into town this afternoon, gave the name Vince Osmond, and made the pasteboards dance. You don't ask overmany questions west of the Mississippi, 'specially of gamblers as to where they were last."

"It's not generally considered polite east of the river, either," Jessie allowed.

"Glad to get him without askin' questions," Chenault added. He was over working the combination of a tall iron safe, now, here in what Jessie surmised was his office. A flat table and several chairs were grouped in the middle, a file cabinet and ledger case along the rear, between the one window and a door. The safe took up a near corner. Chenault quickly secured the sack in the safe, locked his office, and took Jessie cross-hall through the other door.

These were his private quarters, Jessie saw upon entering—two rooms, similar to his office in size but without rear doors, connected by a curtained archway. The second room was Chenault's bedchamber, where he retired to freshen up while Jessie glanced about the front room. It was tastefully outfitted with paintings, books and comfortable furniture, but lacked doilies and brick-a-brac and other feminine graces abhorred by confirmed bachelors. There was, instead, an elegance to the smallish dining table, which was covered with linen and arranged for two, with candlesticks and a vase of wildflowers . . . and that elegance certainly was evident as well in Neal, Jessie thought, as he emerged wearing an unwrinkled shirt and neat tie.

Supper was a catered affair, courtesy of the restaurant staff. The food was standard menu fare—nothing exotic, but prepared and served with a careful awareness of who's boss. The boss had a private stash of select wines, as is a boss' perquisite, and each course was well lubricated with a different variety of vintage wine.

Supper flowed well. Chenault, his manner gracious and outgoing, his conversation shrewdly probing, confirmed within Jessie her initial impressions: He was a smart, knowledgeable fighter motivated by the thrill of new challenges, the wonder of strange fields of endeavour, and confident in his ability to gamble and master any encounter. Not surprisingly, he exuded an innate enthusiasm, a relish for life while he was at his prime, an undercurrent of excitement which Jessie found infectious, seductively alluring.

There was no question that Chenault found Jessie alluring. As an inquisitive sort, he was a profound admirerer of nature's bounties, especially bountiful females such as Jessie. She was independent, for sure, an island whose spectacular terrain made his palms itch to explore. Her approaches could be hazardous, and beaching might spark a native uprising, but still, he was tempted to tackle the conquest, sensing rich rewards if he could ever plant his flag. He doubted he'd locate any virgin growth left, but he didn't believe he'd find erosion or contamination either, or any pollution, any squalor left by earlier plunderers. Her natural resources appeared well developed but far from fully exploited, he felt, and he'd concentrate his prospecting on the potentially fertile belt of untapped deposits and unplumbed depths in her bush country. Well, maybe. And maybe she'd remain unlanded and untrekked despite his efforts; or she might be posted off-limits, the private game preserve of some wealthy mogul. As it was, she wore a light pearl-gray wool ensemble covering landmarks and navigational points, making even his speculations difficult.

After supper, Chenault stood up with a half-empty bottle and said as a toast: "Let's kill it."

Jessie smiled. "All right, I'll split the split."

They moved to the sofa, chatting casually while the waiter cleaned up the table. Shortly after the waiter departed, the bottle ran dry and Jessie said, "I believe I should say g'night." She stayed put, stuffed and groggy. "G'night."

"You said it," Chenault drained his glass, then reached across and grasped Jessie's hand, helping to boost them both to their feet. They stood that way for a few moments. Jessie wasn't thinking about the etiquette or propriety of it, but rather how she'd grown to like him increasingly over the evening.

She slid her hand free then, insisting, "I really must go."

"Absolutely. G'night, Jessie."

"Good night."

Chenault bent as though to give Jessie a chaste goodnight peck. And she raised her chin to offer her lips for the same. But the kiss that developed was anything but a chaste peck—her mouth opened willingly beneath his, to the surprise of them both. Chenault encircled her waist with his hands and tugged her closer to him. Tentatively her arms began to work their way around him, and then their bodies were rubbing against each other while their mouths worked hungrily.

Jessie broke the kiss, but remained close enough to feel his hard breath against her cheek. "Neal, no. This is silly."

"Afraid?"

"Leaving. I told you, g'night."

"G'night," Chenault replied. He kissed Jessie again, his hand under her chin, pressing her mouth to his.

Jessie was a bit startled to find herself kissing him again, but she was even more astounded by the subtle kick of it. It wasn't demanding or pressuring, or carnal and lusty. It was warm and quite sweet, and it touched a responsive chord in her that made her feel good about being kissed by Neal Chenault. And it felt very natural when he enclosed her in his arms again, their knees touching, their position awkward and tiring. But his lips were on hers and she felt very sensual and yet very protected in his strong yet gentle yearning, and for a moment, she lost herself in the kiss. The tip of her tongue touched his, and she felt a great convulsive shiver go through him, and it melted her. Her arms, possessing a will of their own, went around him, felt the muscles tensing in his back, felt the masculine build of his body, and tightened in a quick, reflexive movement.

Then it was too late. She let her tongue flick against his in his mouth, and the glow of desire was strong in her. The wet mingling made her forget. They were just two people, a man and a woman kissing in a private room, preparing to make love. And with that confession, the last of her reserve drained away. She wanted him. God, how she wanted him!

Chenault cradled her against his chest in an enveloping arm, guiding her across through the curtained archway, into his bedchamber. The bed was full-size—a massive iron and brass frame, with head and tail grilles sporting four brass scrolls and ten brass rosettes, and posts that must have come nigh to clear seventy inches high. Before Jessie could make mention of its size, Chenault picked her up in his strong arms and tossed her sprawling onto its covers.

Before she stopped bouncing, he was alongside her. Jessie started moaning and quivering, squirming as his fingers molded her sensitive breasts and found one of her nipples under the tightness of her suit-jacket and blouse, and teased it into vivid awareness. Then they both knew it was time to remove all hindrances between their yearning bodies.

"I want to," he murmured, "undress you."

Jessie smiled and lay back, enjoying the touch of his dexterous fingers. She leaned one way, then the other, raising her arms to help him remove her jacket. Then her blouse went too, and Chenault smiled as he stared at her thrusting breasts and dark, jutting nipples, giving each a kiss and moving on.

Kneeling and unfastening her skirt, Chenault pushed it over her arching pelvis and down her legs. Jessie helped kick it aside, leaving it with her shoes in a puddle on the mattress. She wasn't wearing the customary petticoat this time; rather, she had on a fine set of pantalettes, made of lace and nearly translucent silk. Chenault had an exquisite view of the golden-red delta between her thighs as he untied the drawstring and eased her pantalettes down her legs.

"Exquisite," he murmured.

Drawing into a prayer position, he bent forward and kissed her upper thigh, worming higher and more toward the inside. When he shifted slightly, she gasped and stiffened in reflex. It had the effect of pushing her deeper into his wet caress, and a shaft of liquid delight shot through her at his moist, open-mouthed touch.

Nude, in a strange bed. Breasts firm, nipples painfully swollen. Her legs open, forced open by his palms. He was doing stunning things to her body, thrilling things which caused her to squirm with tense pleasure. Then, inevitably, he came to her.

Chenault tore off his clothing. Jessie eyed his bare form as appreciatively as he had studied hers. His shoulders were wide, his hips solid, and the muscles across his torso looked firm, though not the rock they must've been when he was a youth. But youth had been made up for by tempered strength, making Neal a prime combination of strength and maturity.

And virility, Jessie noticed with something akin to trepidation.

When he pressed close alongside her, Jessie reveled in the heat of her breasts against his chest, and could feel heat elsewhere at his fondling touch. She gasped when his finger traced up and down the seam of her nether lips, finding the center of her passion with a practiced finger, and pressing and rolling it gently. Sighs and low moans erupted from her mouth, passion sparking through her until she was ready to plead for him to stop teasing. Then he did stop, and she yearned for more.

Backing away, Chenault pushed between her legs. She watched the look on his face as he guided his thick, pulsating manhood forward. She opened her legs wider to him, sprawling and spreading lasciviously. She could feel his staff deep within her moist furrow, throbbing and searching out every fold, every hidden nook and cranny. He paused then, lying upon her and pressing her breasts. Jessie pressed against him in turn, and their eyes met, smiling, as he began pumping—slowly at first, then increasing the tempo of his pistoning flesh, until he was plunging swiftly, forcefully inside.

Jessie placed both hands on his buttocks and urged him still deeper, her lips burning against his again, forming moaning sounds without meaning. He shoved his hips forward, forcing her buttocks to grind against the bed, forcing his turgid member into her aching inner depths. Her pointed nipples stabbed his chest at each new thrust of their loins. Her lips continued to shape sweet, wordless sighs in rhythm with his plunging sword. Her knees bent high, and her ankles climbed his back, allowing him to penetrate more fully, her murmurings beginning to change in tone and pitch as she built toward her climax.

Yet she had not started her climax in earnest; there was still time, she wanted more. Sensing her unleashed yearnings, Chenault levered himself up, let her place her legs above his shoulders, then shoved home once more, swiftly and savagely. In unison they pumped faster, faster, Jessie virtually bent double, her eyes dilated, mouth twisted, muttering incoherently. She felt

Chenault's answering throbs and knew he was rapidly spiraling toward his own release. She strove harder, swifter, to grip him with her moist, moving sheath, intolerable pressure rising in her belly, even as Chenault's rampaging erection erupted deep inside her thirsty flesh.

"Yessss . . ." she hissed, shivering, gritting her teeth, and clenching her eyes closed as her own climax overwhelmed her. Her legs extended ceilingward as her seething loins held ravenously the torrent flooding into her . . . and then they splayed wide and dropped limply on either side of Chenault.

Chenault fell forward, remaining locked between her pulsating thighs. Finally, after a long sigh of contentment, he withdrew, rolling on his side and propping himself on one elbow, smiling. Her eyes met his while she lay in quivering sensation, her flesh drained of energy, yet sensually alive.

"Never have I known a woman like you," Chenault murmured.

Jessie laughed softly. "The Romeo compliment. It's true, everybody's unique. But surely the local ladies aren't suffering from your inattentions."

"My downright neglect, I swear, though I doubt they've greatly suffered. The Rosebud's been my mistress since I bought the ruins, and I've built it, made it work, by not straying and by gambling on long chances. I'd keep it that way, for high stakes, but the Rosebud's done, a sure thing. It makes me almost as much money as the doc or the undertaker, who're doing the big business since the Skeleton Crew hit this section, but it's routine, boring, and I've lost interest. You can buy me out, Jessie."

"No, thanks. Neal, how do you size up the Ghost Raiders?"

"*Rapaces*—ghoulish vultures, feedin' off the dead in more ways than one. They've run at will these past few months, untouched till you shot one. Sheriff Beard

97

showing the costume showed 'em up as meat'n'tater targets, but I don't think it was needed to show anyone they weren't ghosts. White paint on black masks may've duped the very ignorant or superstitious, but it wouldn't take in many sensible folk for long. But when anyone getting in range either dies or's shot to the brink, you can't blame them for growing jumpy. Torchin' Genesee Maddox was an extra fearsome lesson, like they were agin' him special."

"Charlie Wolfe didn't get along with Maddox, did he?"

"Not Genesee; so-so with Caleb, for the sake of Diedre. But him'n'Genesee never got on; their wrangle reached a head last year, when Genesee and some Slash-C hands caught Wolfe beside a fire. A hot iron was in the fire and a Slash-C calf close by with a half-run brand on it. Wolfe claimed he'd just found it while riding home, which's possible, Wolfe having a small spread nearby and often crossing the Slash-C there-abouts. But Genesee swore he'd rode out of the bushes behind Wolfe and caught him redhanded."

"Not much evidence to convict anyone of cinch-ring-ing."

"Jury thought so. Besides, Genesee warned that loos-ening Wolfe was same's branding him a liar. And Wolfe's a hot-tempered young cuss who'd had run-ins with other folks. But the judge wasn't much swayed, I guess, seein' as he gave Wolfe a year—nine months, after good behavior."

"In other words, it was Genesee's testimony that convicted him."

"Right. And Wolfe sure looked murder at Genesee when he was on the witness stand. And, incidently, it wasn't long after Wolfe stopped making hair bridles that Genesee was done in. Funny how things work out, isn't it?"

"Yeah," a harsh voice snapped. "It is."

Jessie and Chenault stiffened upright, staring across the shadowy bedroom. At the archway stood a man with a leveled sawed-off shotgun, the twin muzzles trained on them. Behind him, the curtain was moving as two more men filed through, revolvers ready in hand. All three wore the skull masks of the ghostly raiders.

"Wal, ain't this plumb too bad," the man at the arch gloated. "C'mon, get outta the sack, we're takin' a short trip."

"Let her stay," Chenault responded. "I'll do what you want."

"That's why she's comin' along. Now, let's go, as yuh are!"

Jessie balked. "Only place I go to naked is to bed, Mister."

"Je-sus." The man shrugged. "Make it snappy, an' no tricks."

The other two men snickered. Chenault didn't laugh, though; he was a hapless, vivid pink as he rose from the bed and began to dress.

Jessie averted her face, embarrassed for him, but enraged more than personally ashamed. She attempted to be nonchalant as she slipped on her clothes, ignoring the prurient stares, giving the impression she was simply a good-time gal, unarmed and defenseless. She'd fussed to get dressed out of more than mere modesty, though; she wanted to avoid being searched. Still, a fat lot of good it did being able to spring her derringer against three armed men at a distance.

Covered by the men, they were directed out through the front room, and halted at the hall door. "Go across and unlock your office," the shotgunner ordered Chenault. "Soon's it's clear, we're coming over, got it?"

Chenault nodded, licking dry lips as he opened the door.

"So's you won't forget, we got your wench," the shotgunner said. Another man pressed in behind Jessie.

His rough palm clamped over her mouth, forcing her head back, his gun hand pressing the muzzle of his revolver to her exposed throat. "You get different idears, buster, you get her dead."

Face paling, Chenault hastened to unlock his office door. Checking up the hall, he gave a nod, and the men hustled Jessie across before anyone chanced to see them. Lamp lighted, door relocked, Chenault was prodded to the safe while Jessie was told, "Go sit still, hands on the table, and don't talk. Nothin' worse'n a yammery female."

Soon as Chenault ran the combination and unbolted the safe, he was ordered to sit next to Jessie. He obeyed; there was nothing else to do. The men with revolvers holstered their weapons, squatting at the safe and quickly scooping its contents into Chenault's canvas collection sack. Alongside, the shotgunner stood alert, his eyes and gunbarrels fixed on his captives' hands. What he did not see was Jessie's foot slowly rising under the table until her toe hooked against the far sideboard of the table.

Straightening, their job finished, one man tightened the pucker string of the sack, while the other drew his revolver, asking "Now?"

The shotgunner shook his head. "I got a better idear. Tie an' gag the saloonkeep, and bring his sweetie with us. His spreadin' word of that oughta shake up the wimmen 'round here some."

Holstering, the second man started toward Chenault, fingering a short piece of rope. For a moment he was almost between the shotgunner and the table. Jessie's foot kicked forward and up with all the strength of her bent leg behind it. The table surged into the air, flipped over. Jessie went sideward from her chair.

Both barrels of the shotgun let fly with a deafening roar, but the buckshot charges slammed into the heavy tabletop. By then Chenault was diving to the other side, as surprised as the others but swift on the uptake. Jessie had whipped the derringer out of her jacket pocket, and she took swift aim and triggered. The shotgunner went down, drilled through the heart.

The second man, ducking back from the flying table, clawed out his revolver and swiveled toward Jessie. She fired again, her last shot. The man gave a coughing grunt and pitched headlong, his revolver clattering to the floor. The third man managed to keep hold of the sack while drawing and firing. His slug knocked splinters into Jessie's face as she sprang for cover behind the table, her derringer useless and no other weapon handy. She heard the click of the gunhammer and braced for the man's next bullet.

Gunfire blasted. The bulging sack thudded on the boards, and its masked holder fell over it. Across from Jessie, Chenault crouched with a smoking revolver—the second man's dropped weapon, which he'd snatched up from the floor. Before Jessie could utter a word, he shifted his aim. The table lamp burst into pieces and darkness engulfed the room.

At the same time, the night-shrouded rear window blazed with light. The glass shattered as lead stormed through. Jessie flattened, hearing the hiss of bullets passing overhead, then two fire-lancing reports from Chenault's pistol. Then for a moment they lay motionless, listening intently.

From the hotel lobby was coming a wild pandemonium of shouts, yells, and curses. The office door shook from pounding fists. Trying to block out the noise, Jessie thought she detected the pad of running feet outside the back. Apparently so did Chenault, who scrambled across the room to the rear door and flung it open. Jessie was a pace behind. The sound of footsteps faded down a back alleyway, but now something hit the office door with a prodigious crash.

"Hold it!" Chenault yelled at them. Then he craned

101

out the back, listening with Jessie for another moment. Again the office door was struck by a heavy object. Muttering a curse, Chenault and Jessie stepped inside, heading for the office door. A third blow and it caved open, slamming against the wall.

"Everything's under control," Chenault snapped. "Fetch some light."

The wizened desk clerk hurriedly brought a glowing lamp, as staff and guests crowded around in the hallway, talking and gesturing excitedly. Sheriff Beard then shouldered his way through, bellowing, "Back, get back! You're worse'n stockyard cows!" He slammed the door on the babbling throng.

Chenault told a slightly edited version of the events. Listening, the sheriff glowered at the outlaws as Jessie went removing their hoods.

The man whose revolver Chenault used had a burly, leather-skinned face with thickly-browed eyes set too close together. Besides finding him hog-ugly when she unmasked him, Jessie also saw that her derringer bullet had creased a bleeding furrow across his left temple. It was a wound not unlike the puncher's injury she'd patched at the ranch, and with about the same effect.

"This one's stunned, but he's alive."

"More's the pity," Sheriff Beard muttered. He sent for the doctor, shut the door again on the milling crowd, then began emptying the pockets of the unsavory trio. "Might be something to brand 'em, by name or to some outfit," he explained.

The wounded man moaned when he was searched, thrashing a bit as though starting to regain consciousness. But there was nothing to identify him or the others, nor anything else unusual, until Beard drew from the shotgunner's pocket a small silver rod, about eight inches long, with a smooth round ball forming one end.

"Funny-lookin' doohickey," Chenault commented

when the sheriff handed him the rod. After studying it for a moment, he passed it to Jessie. "Wonder what in creation it is?"

Jessie did not reply directly, although she frowned thoughtfully as she fingered the tapering bit of metal with the ball at its larger end. Then she remarked casually, "I'd like to keep this as a souvenir, I think."

"Reckon you earned your pick, Jessie," Chenault replied cheerfully.

"Can't see how it'd hurt," the sheriff concurred. "I once knew an hombre who'd cut an ear off every gent he ventilated. Had quite a collection—smoked 'em, and lined 'em up on the mantlepiece of his cabin."

Suddenly the wounded outlaw's eyes flew open, and after an instant of confusion, he tried to leap up and escape. The sheriff and Chenault stopped him. The outlaw's dizziness made him fall flat. He shut his eyes, his chest heaving.

"Easy—you ain't goin' nowhere but jail," the sheriff said firmly. "What's your name?"

"Laslo . . . Floyd Laslo, I— To hell with you; I ain't sayin' no more."

Voice hardening, the sheriff began, "Laslo, you're gonna sing like—"

Then the door burst open again and Doc Terwilliger stomped in. "Nabbed us a live ghost, eh?" he said, as he began to examine Laslo. "That's the spirit."

While the doc was treating him, the sheriff set to questioning Laslo. But Laslo refused to talk, occasionally shaking his head or laughing mockingly. Finished, Terwilliger gave a last look at the turban he'd fashioned around Laslo's head, then began repacking his bag.

Laslo sneered at the sheriff. "I'll be free in a night or two, you'll see. Your jail ain't going to hold me."

The doc turned to Beard. "We'd be in bad shape to stop this bunch of raiders if they decided to spring him."

"Count me in," Chenault offered. "I bet the towns-folk—"

"Will be under their beds, shiverin'," Laslo scoffed.

"If that happens, and you get out," the sheriff vowed, "I'll make sure I put a bullet in you before I die."

Jessie looked at the sheriff, surprised at the vehemence in his voice, and she was convinced Beard would do what he said. She wished the answers were as clear, but they seemed as elusive, as ethereal, as phantoms. Nonetheless, she grimly pledged that once Laslo was behind bars, the solution would be forthcoming.

★

Chapter 8

After the funerals of the dead hands and the pathetic bundle of bones, the Slash-C roundup began in earnest.

The crew wanted to construct a ranch cabin for Diedre, but she declared Lok Yuan's bed quarters in the cookshack perfectly suitable, and pitched in as chef during the gather. So Ki and his riders immediately set to combing the brakes and canyons, finding, as Ki suspected they would, plenty of saleable beefs tucked in cool, grassy hideaways. They were an ornery, intractable lot, and gave constant trouble as windies usually do.

"Whoever named that sort of cow 'windies' shore had the right notion," Paul Everts complained at dinner, after a long day of chasing belligerent steers. "I shore am plumb winded."

"Tomorrow we'll hit those thickets to the west and see if we can't run out a few cedar-breakers," Ki told him and the other crewmen.

Paloo groaned. "If there's a worse chore than snakin'

ladino stock from cedar thickets, I dunno what it is!"

"You ought to try busting sea cows down in the Gulf Coast country like I once did," Ki claimed deadpan. "Those sea-lion cows grow fins on their hocks, and when you daub a loop on 'em, they raise a foot and saw the rope in half with a fin."

"Son," Paloo replied severely, "lyin' to a gent my age ain't decent. Them sea-lions don't wear fins on their hoofs, but on the end 'o their tails. They cut the twine by wrappin' their tail around it and giving a quick jerk. You stick to truths hereafter and folks'll think better of yuh..."

Sweating, swearing, the crew continued to toil in the dust and heat. From all over the range, scattered cattle were choused home in close herd, and carefully guarded. As a further precaution, Ki wanted to check the route they'd use to run the herd to the construction camp, and consulted the waddie most familiar with the area, Jingo Paloo.

"Only way we can drive them through the hills," Paloo told him, "is by way of Perdition Gap. A mule can't hardly cross that upended section elsewise, and cows never. The Gap is it, and it's the devil's stampin' grounds."

In the dim hours before dawn, Ki and old Paloo quietly left the Slash-C and headed northeast. Before long Ki was ready to agree with Paloo that the Gila hills were practically impossible to negotiate. They were a jumble of arroyos, gorges, jagged rimrocks, cliffs, and precipitous slopes. Ravine emptied into ravine, and the striated walls were honeycombed with caves and crevices. The wild confusion was intensified by the dense growth that choked the depressions and covered the banks.

"Just the same, I'd bet the raiders have a hideout somewhere up in here," Ki remarked to Paloo as they rode along. "They know how to get to it and cover their tracks. Their boss must be as familiar as you with the area, Jingo, and that gives him a decided advantage over most everyone else, who're new."

Morning was growing late when they entered Perdition Gap. It was indeed "the devil's stampin' grounds," with its towering splintered walls and gloomy, boulder-strewn floor. So rugged and stony was the floor that practically no growth could find rootage in the scanty soil. Waterless and barren, the mighty cleft bored into the beetling, craggy hills that were themselves a scene of arid desolation.

"One good thing about it, though," Ki noted, "there's no place for a rustling stampede, such as was pulled in Bleaker Canyon."

"Uh-huh, so far," Paloo allowed. "And them Skull Killers would be tempted to wide-loop our sizeable-growin' herd, or I'm a heap mistook."

Mile after mile they rode, with the rock walls slowly drawing together until the Gap was but a narrow defile swathed in shadow. They had covered perhaps half the distance between the Slash-C and the construction camp when the first break came in the grim barriers of stone. Leftward yawned a narrow, overgrown side cut. Across on the opposite side of the Gap, the growth continued, crowding up against the east wall of the narrow trail for several hundred yards, then thinning to a straggle, to be replaced by the monotonous litter of boulders.

Ki reined in and stared at the brush-clogged mouth of the side cut. "I've a hunch if the raiders tried anywhere, it'd be here. Let's take a gander."

With difficulty they pushed their mounts through the thick brush that filled the mouth of the side cut. For perhaps a hundred feet the brush grew closely together, and higher than the head of a mounted man, their tops interlacing to form a tangle of grayish green. Then gradually the growth petered out, until it almost ceased altogether in the center of the gorge, although it still grew thick along the walls. Down the center could be seen a path, little more than a game track. And scarring its surface were prints of horses' irons.

"Jingo, where's this lead to?"

"I'd reckon it'd run down onto the flats to the west," Paloo hazarded. "Ain't never rode through it, and didn't figger anyone had. Shore nuthin' to make anyone want to, far as I can tell."

"Nor as far as anyone else could tell," Ki admitted, dismounting to study the hoofmarks closely. "But it's been used going and coming, a good week or more ago. Well, let's get back to the Gap and see if there's any more likely spots between here and the camp."

They continued to follow the winding Gap until the sides fell back and the trail reached the edge of a long plateau of slopes and knolls. A mile or more beyond loomed a bristle of crags thrusting from the main rise of hills to the east and north. There they glimpsed the dark, eroded gorge of the Blue River. At a distant point along its whitewater course was the construction site of the dam, bustling with labor, belching exhaust from steam machinery, its bankside camp a field of temporary structures, supply dumps, and rail sidings.

"Going all the way to the camp?" Paloo asked.

Ki shook his head. "Don't want to be seen there. In fact, we're heading back around about the hills to the west, not through the Gap, just to make sure we keep out of sight and don't tip our hand."

"It'll be plumb dark before we get home," Paloo replied disgustedly.

"So much the better. Let's go."

It was, in truth, long after dark when they arrived at the ranch.

"That side cut is the only spot there'd be much chance to try anything," Ki remarked to Paloo as they shucked the rigs from their weary horses. "The Gap there is so narrow and brushy that our point, swing, and flank riders will have to pull back and join the drag riders. Our whole crew will be bunched behind the herd when driving past the cut. You'll have to be on your toes, Jingo, and'll be taking a risk of stopping lead. Willing?"

"The bullet ain't run that can do me in," Paloo declared stoutly. "Right now I got so much lead in my carcass it'd pay to mine me. The only time I was ever in real risk of expirin' was once when I'd so many bullet-holes in me, I like to've starved to death from leakin' out my vittles."

"To hear you stick to truths, Jingo, is pure inspiration . . ."

The next morning Jessie paid a visit to the ranch. After a pleasant chat with Diedre, she conferred privately with Ki, exchanging news and views.

Since their last talk following the inquest, Jessie had received two telegrams, which she gave Ki to read. One was from Starbuck headquarters, answering her queries precisely and for the most part sufficiently. A few unsatisfactory points, such as "person you described cannot be traced nor is known to New Mexico or Texas authorities," had prompted Jessie to send for further information from Starbuck. The second cable was a reply from J. J. Houglum, concessionaire manager of the dam construction project, whose message was laconic, but brought a chuckling groan from Ki: BRING MOO THE MERRIER.

Jessie related to Ki the robbery attempt at the Rosebud. Floyd Laslo remained in jail, under armed guard while awaiting the circuit judge, who was due next month. He still wouldn't talk, so Sheriff Beard was refusing entry to all but a trusted handful, fearing he'd unwittingly let in the wrong guy, and lose Laslo.

"The sheriff's right," Jessie asserted. "Until Laslo fingers the gang, nobody can be discounted. Neal and I never suspected the waiter who served our supper, but he's gone and so's his key, and the door must've been unlocked for the bandits to've snuck in on us later. They'd inside help, all right. They knew the Rosebud had made a good profit, and when to hit Neal after his last collection, and had a backup in the alley to take care of any interruptions. A smooth and nervy bunch, Ki, but greedy weak. They can't keep their mitts off a dead man's personals," Jessie added cryptically, and showed Ki the peculiar silver rod with a ball at the end that had been taken from the shotgunner.

Ki examined it thoughtfully, then returned it to Jessie. "Yeah, that's the tie-up," he said as she slipped it into her pocket. "But where in blazes is the bastard we've got to run down . . . ?"

The following dawn, the drive got under way. The herd ran to plenty, bigger and in better condition than even Ki had dared to hope for.

"With the money these cows will bring, you'll be sitting pretty for quite a spell," he told Diedre the night before the drive.

North by west rolled the welter of shaggy backs and tossing horns. The trail crew shoved the herd along fast to get them off their home range, where they evinced a greater tendency to stray. Point-men rode near the head of the herd to direct its course. About a third of the way back from the point-men were the swing riders, where the herd began to bend in case of a change of course. Another third of the way back were the flank riders, who blocked the cattle from wandering sideward. At the rear were the tail or drag riders, swearing at the heat, the dust, and the stragglers.

Since the drive was a short one, there was no remuda or chuckwagon along. Ordinarily the trail boss would have ridden ahead of the herd to survey the ground and search out water and grazing; but with the expectation of delivering the herd before nightfall, these duties were unnecessary. The designated trail boss, Jingo Paloo, rode with the drag men behind the herd.

Paloo had with him a little over half of the Slash-C outfit. The others, armed with rifle and revolver, and with Ki at their lead, had ridden away from the spread during the dark hours of the previous night, circling through the hills to arrive unseen at the mouth of the side-cut in Perdition Gap.

Old Paloo was watchful and alert, his heavy rifle resting across his saddle bow, his rheumy eyes roaming the terrain on either side of the ambling herd. His riders were also tense and expectant, and there was little of the chaffing and skylarking that usually is part of the beginning of a trail. The punchers knew they were risking their lives, if their foreman's hunch should prove correct, and their mood was correspondingly serious.

Into Perdition Gap flowed the herd, not liking it at all, bawling at the dimness and the hard tracking. The cows had a tendency to mill, but the point riders herded in those attempting to fan out, and the drag men forced the stragglers to keep pace with the main body.

Darker and darker grew the gorge, and closer and closer the black cliffs drew together. The querulous bellowing of the cattle echoed drearily from the towering walls. Their hoofs drummed loudly on the rocky floor. The crew struggled to keep the herd moving, crouching low in their saddles, peering anxiously ahead into the deepening murk.

The van of the herd reached the mouth of the ominous side-cut, and rumbled past it. The main body jostled on with clacking horns and rolling eyes. The point, swing, and flank riders had dropped back until the entire crew was riding behind the herd, keeping as far apart as possible, shielding themselves behind their horses' necks. They gripped the bridles with sweating palms and strained their eyes ahead.

With nerve-shattering unexpectedness, the "expected" happened. A volley of shots cracked from the brush-choked side-cut, and lead sizzled about the Slash-C riders. As one, they curveted their horses and galloped madly back the way they had come. The herd bawled with terror and began to mill.

Out of the brushy mouth of the cut streamed skull-hooded men, hooting derisively as they hurled bullets after the fleeing cowboys. Their whoops of triumph changed to howls of shock as from the dark thicket on the opposite side of the trail there burst a salvo of gunfire. Under that first thunderous barrage three saddles were emptied. The survivors whirled, dazed with alarm, ducking and dodging as lead stormed around them, and for a moment they seemed to hesitate, as confused as the floundering cattle.

Some tried to rally, firing wildly at the growth where nothing moved, but from which the deadly fusillade continued to pour. Then the Slash-C trail crew, yelling and swearing, rushed back, charging with careless abandon, the cavernous gorge reverberating with the blasts of their weapons. The outlaws, caught in a crossfire, were not slow in turning their frantic horses and seeking cover. Two more bit the dust, and another choked with pain as a bullet smashed his arm. Their compadres tore madly for the shelter of the side-cut, firing as they fled, screaming in agony and dropping in their tracks.

Last of all was a tall man on a splendid black horse. With word and gesture, he urged his henchmen away from the fast-snapping, brutal gun-trap, while covering their retreat with broadsides of bullets into the thicket.

Hunkering within the brush, Ki aimed his Winchester .44-40 at the tall leader, his black eyes gleaming as he squeezed the trigger. He caught the man nearest the leader, when the leader zigged and the other man zagged at the last possible instant. The man toppled against the leader's black horse, which shied and almost unseated the leader, who hurriedly slewed the horse about, out of Ki's gun-sights. Before Ki could draw a bead again, the outlaw boss had vanished into the protective screen of undergrowth.

"After them!" Ki shouted. His men sprinting with him, he raced to where their horses were tethered, some little distance off in the scrub.

The Slash-C punchers who had staged the ambush mounted in furious haste and launched from the thicket. They were immediately engulfed in the churning herd. Try as they might, it took precious minutes for them to disentangle from the bellowing, blundering cattle.

"Take the herd on to the camp!" Ki yelled to Paloo and the trail crew as he led his party into the side-cut. They tore through the brush, heedless of thorns and whipping branches, and when they bulged from the final straggle of bushes, there was no sight of the skull-masked rustlers. But there was only one way they could have gone. Neck and neck the pursuing riders thundered down the cut, which presently began to curve. Ki called a word of caution:

"Easy, now! They might hole up and lay for us around one of these bends!"

At a swift pace he led his men, watchful, alert, peering and listening. The turns became more frequent, the cut narrowing until the floor was barely a hundred yards wide. The perpendicular rock walls were replaced by slopes bristling with chaparral, studded with boulders, soaring upward to torn and ragged rimrocks far above. The bed of the cut was choked with dead-looking growth, between which the path ran so narrow that the riders were forced to proceed in single file. So ominous, indeed, was the terrain that Ki slowed the pursuit to a jog.

Suddenly he uttered an exclamation and reined in. Directly ahead of them a cloud of smoke was boiling

113

up. "They've fired the brush to hold us off!"

One of the crew gave a yelp. "There's smoke risin' behind us, too!"

"We're trapped!" yammered another puncher. "We'll be roasted alive!"

"Shut up!" Ki snapped, glancing over his shoulder at the billowing ocher cloud. "We're not done yet, but we've got to move fast. This brush is dry as tinder. We've got to make it up the slope to the rimrock."

"C'mon!" shouted the frightened cowpoke, wrenching his horse toward the relatively gentle bank on the left.

But his bridle was seized in Ki's iron grip. "Not that way, you damned fool! That's the easy way—the way they'd figure we'd take. Mount that slope and we'll get potshot like sitting brush hens! Turn right."

"We can't ne'er make it up that wall!"

"You'll make it, or burn!" Ki countered grimly. "Get going! The fire's closing fast, both ways!"

Up the steep sag they sent their horses, the animals slipping and floundering and giving protesting snorts. Already the smoke was drifting about them in acrid clouds. They could hear the crackle and roar of the flames consuming the dry growth. As they climbed farther up the slope, they could see the cut was a seething welter of fire to the east and west, spreading swiftly up the slopes and threatening to overtake them before they could reach the sanctuary of the rimrock.

Faster and faster scrambled the now thoroughly terrified horses, their riders urging them to greater efforts with voice and spur. But faster still the fire squeezed the already dangerously narrow lane of escape. They reached a point that was comparatively free of growth, studded with boulders and composed largely of loose shale that rolled and slipped under the horses' hoofs. Something sang over their heads and ricocheted off a stone.

"Gawd a'mighty, they's shootin' at us!"

"Never mind! Move!" Ki shouted. Holding his Slash-C mount firmly in check, he kept to the rear of the crew, encouraging the weaker, herding the stragglers toward the summit.

But as more slugs peppered around them, Ki reined in and dismounted, sliding his carbine from its boot as he did so. Bracing his back against a boulder, he gazed across to the far slope. The fierce draft raging down the cut held the dense smoke clouds low, and visibility was fairly good.

A bullet spatted viciously against the stone scant inches from his head, showering him with stinging fragments. Motionless, he continued to stare across the clouded cut. Another bullet struck, but this time Ki spotted a telltale whitish puff which gushed from the growth. The carbine leaped to his shoulder, his steady eyes glancing along the sights. He levered shot after shot into the brush beneath the smoke plume.

At his fourth shot, the growth was violently agitated. Something black pitched from it and rolled down the slope. Ki chambered again just in case, then tensed, watching and waiting. But no more slugs whined across. The growth remained still, silent.

Satisfied that only one raider had climbed up there to keep a lookout, Ki turned and sprang into his saddle. Booting his carbine, he sent his horse lunging after his crew, who were now far ahead.

The heat was stifling, the smoke so thick he could hardly breathe. His ears rang with the roar of the conflagration, and as he peered ahead, he suddenly saw a tongue of flame waver directly in front of him. It vanished, to be supplanted by another, broader one. Then the growth ahead was displaced by a flickering wall of fire, closing him off from escape.

Ki bent low, shielding his face with his arms while coaxing the horse onward. Whinnying, panic-stricken, his mount plunged into the curtain of flame. Ki gasped as the fiery fingers bit at his flesh. His temples throbbed, and his chest was constricting. All around him roared and crackled the burning brush. Hot brands showered down upon him, and his nostrils were choked by stinging ash. He could feel the horse stagger, reel, flounder as its hoofs slipped on the stones. He held it to its footing with an iron grip on the reins, calling rough encouragement.

Another mighty effort, and an explosive snort from the spooked horse, and the fire was behind them. Through the swirling smoke, Ki could see his punchers prodding their mounts up the rimrock, casting worried glances over their shoulders. A moment more and Ki was beside them, beating out the fire that smoldered on his garments. On top of the rimrock, with the fire raging below them, they pulled up in comparatively clear air.

Ki stared down into the inferno that was the cut. "Well, they took that trick, but they didn't get the herd."

"Didn't get us, either," a puncher exulted. "Just the same, I reckon to eat my chuck raw from here on. I don't want e'er to see another fire!"

Ki had a few blisters on his hand, and his horse had lost some patches of hair. The Slash-C crew was smoke-blackened and red-eyed, and some had sustained slight burns from flying brands, but aside from these minor discomforts, nobody was the worse for his harrowing experience. However, their ride from there was a thirsty and arduous one. It was long past dusk when, after an exhausting scramble along the rimrock and down the long slopes of the hills, they came to the construction camp.

Ki at once repaired to the office of the stockyard superintendent, where he found Jingo Paloo anxiously awaiting him.

"Didn't have a mite of trouble the rest of the drive," Paloo informed him. "Son, you shore gave them hellions a-plenty. We looked over the batch that were downed there in the Gap, mean-looking cusses, but nobody recognized any of 'em. I brung their skull-masks along in case you'd care to have 'em."

The superintendent was gratified to get the herd. "We needed 'em. These rockbusters won't work without lots of whiskey and meat. I got 'em all weighed up, and here's a voucher that can be cashed at the bank in Whitewash. Say, you must have a stand with the Old Man—J. J. Houglum, the manager. We got word from him to buy every head brought in, and that's the first time he agreed to accept stuff in small lots without guarantee of future shipments. Do you know him personal?"

"Never met the man," Ki replied, adding enigmatically, "but I believe we may be aquainted with the same lady."

The combined Slash-C crew soon began their weary return trek. It was deep into the night when they finally arrived, exhausted, at the ranch. Diedre was up waiting with coffee and grub, and stared wide-eyed at the blackened, disheveled riders pulling in. Not long afterwards, they were flopping in their bunks and pounding their ears.

The bunkhouse was a resonant black cave of grumblings and snores when Ki awakened later, needing to take a piss. In just his shirt and jeans, he quietly padded outside and across the yard to the outhouse, a small but powerful two-holer concealed by tall brush.

Stepping from the outhouse to return, Ki halted at the door, hearing a faint scratching noise from beyond the brush. When it ceased a moment later, he chalked it up to a foraging rodent, and hastened on from the outhouse. Following the footpath that wound through the brush, he cleared the last turn and reached the yard at a quickening pace—

—And collided with Diedre, who was rushing from

the brushy fringe, clad in only her peignoir now. He almost brained her before recognizing who it was.

"Don't shoot!" she gasped.

"I'm not armed."

"Well, you never can be too sure about that." She snuggled up against him, like a cat seeking affection, her voice faltering. "I . . . I hoped it was you. I felt so alone and scared till y'all got back, Ki." Her chin trembled, a portent of tears. "You must think me such a sissy."

"No, and don't you think it. Everyone lets his hair down now and then, and after all you've suffered, nobody deserves to more than you."

"Not me. I won't buckle," she insisted, eyes misty. "Damn, I wish I was a man."

"If you were," Ki said, growing chary, "a lot of other men would be sorely upset."

"Not a lot; that's mean of you." She pressed her face against his chest. Ki heard her sob, and even while calling himself a sucker, he placed an arm around and patted her shoulder to comfort her. He conjured up things to say that might dampen her creeping ardor, but she kissed him before he could open his mouth. It shut him up, too, potently more persuasive than anything he could say. Hell, he was convinced, so he kissed her back. She returned the kiss, and things developed into a fast, torrid volley of lips for the next few minutes.

Diedre broke their embrace then, as abruptly as she'd begun. She eyed Ki with a kind of frenzy. "We can't stay here."

Ki nodded. Anyone in the yard, in the bunkhouse, or outhouse-bound might see them. *Every*one would, knowing *his* luck. And if they did, he'd a hunch it'd cause one helluva big hash hereabouts. "But where?"

Diedre was barefooted, and she was quick on her toes in more ways than one. Pulling Ki by the hand, she ran, favoring her sprained ankle, across the yard, and darted into the grove that separated the yard and the horse field. The ground was typical summer drypan, rougher than a cob, and as Ki followed along, he wondered if Diedre had a penchant for stand-up sexing.

They continued, threading their way through the tangle of rocks, brush, and trees, until they reached a clump of boulders. As they moved between the boulders, Ki noticed grass growing in tufts at their feet, an indication of a spring or a tank. Once within the screening rock, he saw that it encircled a small patch, which bordered a stream-bed and the bank of a shallow pool. There was nary a drop of water in either one. Sometime, for some reason, their flows dried up, Ki surmised, but enough ground seepage remained to sustain the greenery.

Diedre then showed him a different nature lesson. She backed him up against one of the boulders, squeezing so close to him that he could feel the hotly beating pulse of her. They began kissing again, and as often as Ki kissed her, Diedre paid back the kiss, with wanton interest—until finally she drew away and stood in front of him. Humming provocatively, she pulled her peignoir over her head, her pert breasts swaying gracefully as she tossed her gown high, letting it float to the grass.

Buck-ass naked, she cuddled closer. "What's keeping you?" she purred, grabbing Ki's rope belt and tugging.

Ki felt the tug all the way down through his taut loins. Diedre crushed her body to his, kissing him with hot, moist urgency. She helped him out of his shirt and jeans, baring him to the cool night air, then lay stretched out on the grass, watching, her arms spread wide and her legs slightly apart.

"Make it," she whispered, "make it as good as last time."

What was made was a hard, quick union. Ki lunged deep into her in sheer lust. Diedre moaned in her eagerness and pushed her pelvis upward in an arc, to devour

119

him, deep and hot, sliding into her belly. Faint cries of animal pleasure rose from her throat, her face contorting with desire, her mouth moving hungrily, her thighs rhythmically squeezing around Ki's pumping flesh. They were no longer aware of anything but the incredible sensations of the moment. Ki quickened his thrusts, searing and pulsating, and the exquisite agony of approaching orgasm caused Diedre to squirm beneath him.

"Ohhhh . . ." she cried, humping faster and faster against him. Ki was aware only of the magnificent pressure building inside him, and of the friction of their bodies as they heaved against each other. He came so violently that for an instant he was unaware that Diedre too was ponding, squeezing her inner muscles in tempo with his pulsing ejections. She circled her legs around him, locking her ankles, bucking upward with her hips, thighs, and buttocks, and claimed the last drops of joy there between her legs.

Slowly Ki settled down over her soft, warm body. He lay, crushing her breasts and belly with his weight, until his immediate satiation began to wane. He rolled from her then, and gently stroked her quivering breasts.

She smiled at him with lazy, satisfied eyes. "You'll get me going again."

"Great, but not now. We should be getting back."

"'Great, but not now.' In a minute, Ki—let me enjoy another minute."

"Okay, just one." He stretched close alongside, telling himself he'd keep to that, alert against slip-ups.

He fell asleep instantly.

He awoke with a start awhile later. It was still dark, but he didn't know the time and didn't much care other than it was goddamn *late*. Diedre was sleeping alongside him, looking strangely young and vulnerable with her face relaxed and her lips softly parted.

"Christ," he muttered, rising and hurriedly dressing.

120

"Wake up," he called gently. "We've got to get a move on."

"Later," she replied woozily. But within a minute she was on her feet, yawning and stretching. "My, it certainly is later," she said, looking disappointed as she retrieved her peignoir. She was still smoothing it out when they started back to the bunkhouse. She looked fresh and dangerously eager for more.

As they were approaching the bunkhouse, Ki said, "It looks like nothing's happened, nobody's the wiser. Let's keep it that way."

She slowed, her hips rubbing his thighs, her breath a hiss in his ear. "Yes, we better. They'll kill you if they find out." Then giving Ki a peck on his cheek, she hurried to the cookshack and vanished inside.

Ki began heading for the bunkhouse door, shaking his head. Sooner or later, he was sure, that vixen would get some idiot killed. God, and all he'd wanted to do was go take a leak! At this point, he just hoped that when he got back in bed, nothing more would disrupt his sleep.

Chapter 9

Earlier that same night, along about the time Ki and his crew were returning to the Slash-C, Jessie had been heading for the Rosebud in company of the delegates.

Her intention was to retire—alone. She was weary, and anyhow Neal was busy. Back at dusk when she'd left the hotel, Chenault had confided that there was a surprise development of a private yet promising nature, that figured to keep him tied up for who knew how long. Even if he'd been free then, however, she still would've gone with the delegates. For despite—or, rather, due to—all the disruptive havoc, Jessie was more interested than ever in the dam project.

The gala ceremony remained slated for tomorrow, assuming no calamities or strikes over unpaid wages. Held this evening was one of the last preliminary functions, a speech by Special Engineer Norkensington on area geology and agronomy. From the Gila to the border, the land was eroded by flash floods, yet the soil was left parched with little surface water, artesian wells being used instead. But in the rainy season the grass spread thick, and the cottonwoods of the washes and the cedars of the mesas grew verdant, testifying to the fact that the earth was not barren, only extremely dry. The simple remedy was to control river flow, and irrigate consistently. Once again Jessie was reminded just how important the Blue River dam would be directly to the Basin, and progressively throughout the territory.

The speech over, the delegates dragged the session on and on, windily digressing, until Norkensington brusquely showed them out. Since their meeting was at the construction project's town quarters, a restored foursquare house down past the livery stable, they had only a short stretch to walk back up to the Rosebud. They kept on blithering, which grated on Jessie almost as much as had their patronizing air upon greeting her return to the fold tonight.

By now they had learned of the Ghost Raiders, of course, though not of her involvement. They hadn't gone berserk, as Governor Cardwell feared, but blandly dismissed the gang as a Halloween rabble that the local law could handle. Indeed, there'd been nary a sign of the bunch since Floyd Laslo had been locked up—or so it appeared; nobody was aware yet of Ki's clash with the rustlers—and they fancied that Laslo must be the boss honcho, whose thugs had deserted him. Or if not, an inspired second opinion contended that because of the delegates' own commanding presence here, "maybe they're reformed."

Jessie entertained no such notions. Nor did the local law, she saw, casting a long eye up at the jail across the street. Night blurred the fringe details, but the front was spotlit by a glaring lantern rigged up under the overhang. Sheriff Beard was locked inside, no doubt, while out below the lantern, Deputy Nudelman sat with his chair against the door, gripping a vintage single-shot

Peabody, frowning suspiciously, and peering intently about.

Well, he was trying. But it was like searching for a particular tick in a flock of black sheep. The street was dark, save for the lantern and the ruddy lamp-glow filtering through dirt- and smoke-rimed window panes; it was alive with range-garbed rowdies and laborers in corduroys and laced boots, jostling one another on the narrow boardwalks. Jessie listened to their drawling laughter and spasmodic profanity with detached but alert curiosity. To her, searching was similar to stringing beads: The bead of a word or incident led to another and then another until accident or violence tied the loose ends together in a knot. And she could never tell when or where she'd catch one of those beads—or the violence.

It was violence, hitting with a sudden vengeance.

A commotion abruptly arose some distance beyond the jail. Staring ahead, Jessie and the startled delegates saw that up by the bank building, men were yelling, a dog was barking, and people were turning and craning all along the street. Running pell-mell from up that way, a muscular laborer with protruding eyes barreled down the street and lunged toward the jail, waving his arms.

A delegate beside Jessie looked reprovingly. "Never a dull moment in Whitewash, is there, Miss Starbuck?"

"Wouldn't be home without it," she replied blithely. Then she added, "But this one sounds like more than the usual rumpus. Maybe we better find out."

For all their disapproval, the delegates hustled right spritely up the street.

Ahead at the jail, Jessie noticed, a confrontation sprang up the instant the man got there. Nudelman sat unbudging from his duty leaning against the door, and glowered at the raging, fist-shaking man. Without warning, then, the door wrenched open, and Nudelman pitched backwards in his chair, boots rearing, just as

Sheriff Beard came barging out. Nudelman's flustered yelp was drowned by the sheriff's bellow as he sprang clumsily aside to avoid his deputy. Nudelman struck with a jarring, tumbling crash against the floor, a mushrooming gust of dislodged dust and grit geysering out the doorway. The man vaulted across Nudelman, who was flailing flat in his busted chair, and the next second the door slammed shut.

A second or two after that, the door flew wide again. The man rushed out with Sheriff Beard, who was carrying a Dietz tubular hand lantern, and they tore up the street. Nudelman appeared with his rifle and another chair, locked the door, and resumed his post, scowling as if suffering from ten ingrown toenails.

Hurrying on by the jail, Jessie focused on Sheriff Beard as he neared the single-story brick bank. With the pop-eyed man alongside, gesturing, the sheriff veered to the left side of the building and down a narrow alley that cut back between the bank and the side of a ramshackle saloon next door. Angling that way, Jessie and the delegates joined the crowd converging on the bank, others behind shoving close on their heels, those in front milling and braying words that gradually evolved into a sort of chant:

"Neal Chenault is dead! Neal Chenault is dead!"

Jessie halted, uncertain, apprehensive.

"Hey, that's my foot, Miss Starbuck! We can't stop here!"

She ignored the grousing delegate, but, incited by his last words, she plowed on through the crush with a fierce impulse not to stop, compelled to go refute the clamor, to prove Chenault was alive as he *must* be. The delegates soon dropped behind, engulfed, and a moment more of determined thrusting brought Jessie before the alley entrance. Onlookers were boiling around, peering constantly down the black pathway where more spectators were crammed, gandering and yammering.

126

Forging ahead, Jessie entered the pitch-dark maw and pressed along for a number of feet before glimpsing the light. It was the faint glow of the sheriff's lantern, casting above the throng, glimmering lightly on the arch of an inset doorway near the rear of the bank. Shouldering, wedging, she bored through fervidly, refusing to admit her fear or accept the possibility, until finally she reached the entry and squeezed to the front.

The alley was clear for the width of the doorway, and mobbed on each side. In the cramped space were the pop-eyed man and three co-workers, standing to one side looking nervously concerned, often glancing sourly across at Charlie Wolfe. In a defiant stance with arms akimbo, Wolfe flashed a cold eye right back; and yet, Jessie sensed, his belligerency seemed more pensive than sullen, as if his bold front was shaken and he was, at heart, worried pissless.

Midway crouched Sheriff Beard, studying the curled-up body of a man.

Her view was blocked by the sheriff, but after a moment he started to straighten, shining his lantern on the body for a last once-over. As he did so, Jessie craned to see, faltering, "Is he . . .?"

"Yep." He stiffened, then, and turned from the body to face Jessie somberly. "Now, Miz Starbuck, this's kinda raw meat for delicate natures."

As he was cautioning her, Jessie took a cursory view of the body. She didn't bother to argue; in fact, she heartily agreed. The victim was not for the squeamish of either sex; his face was waxy, pallid, and blood-smudged, his body strangely deflated and wallowing in blood—his blood, which had spewed out in a torrent from his knife-slit throat. Ear to ear. So deep that his neck was severed almost to his spinal column. When he had dropped, draining out his life in pumping spurts, his head had twisted grotesquely from his trunk, and now

127

lay displaying flesh like the crimson inner gills of a large fish.

And yes, God yes, it was Neal Chenault.

Jessie felt the gorge rising in her throat, and her knees threatened to buckle from the horror and anguish that weighed heavy on her mind. She braced a hand against the brick wall to steady herself, and after a deep breath and a swallow, she told the sheriff firmly, "I'm sticking."

With a slight shrug, he turned to regard the four laborers. "So you say you heard Chenault cry out, izzat right?"

"Everyone in the bar did, Sheriff," the pop-eyed man answered, thumbing at the saloon next door. "It sliced through that flimsy ol' wall, a screamin' banshee what shook us by the roots of our hairs. We'uns were just dumb enough or drunk enough to stampede out to see what 'n hell, and found Chenault lyin' like you sees him, deader'n a mackerel, in a lake o' blood."

"Nothing else, you're positive?"

"Him," another laborer declared, pointing at Wolfe.

The sheriff nodded. "Besides him. A knife, or a—a whatever."

"Clues, you mean." The pop-eyed man shook his head. "No sound or sight of anyone else, an' nothin' in the alley. We checked, just afore everybody piled in. Then I come got you, while m'pals made sure Wolfe didn't stray."

"You did good, real good," the sheriff said. He focused, scowling, on Wolfe. "Charlie, now's no time for smart-alecky answers, an' if you—"

"Hey, here comes Hevis!" someone shouted. A moment later Lucian Hevis shoved through to the doorway, wearing his bowler and a staid dark suit, his spare features a trifle more agitated and moody than before. Then he caught a glimpse of Neal Chenault, and his expression knotted as though he'd been stiffed cod-liver oil.

128

His legs wobbled, and his hands fluttered as he averted his face, gagging. *"Awk, awk . . ."*

The guy alongside moved out of range. "We best get the doc!"

"Doc's been rousted and'll be along," the sheriff responded.

"I've a little flask of whiskey," a short, rotund townsman offered. "I use it to ward off mosquitoes."

The sheriff gave a snort. "There ain't a mosquito within a hundred miles of Whitewash, Hilliard, and you know it." Again he eyed the banker, who was shakily recuperating on his own, and spoke sympathetically. "Lucian, if you feel able to, have you any notion what Chenault was doing back here?"

"I urged that he let me accompany him to the bank. I—I argued, begged him," Hevis responded dazedly. It was a momentary lapse, and as he was wiping his brow with a linen handkerchief, his distraught confusion was wearing off with his shock. "Yes. Well. Neal refused, I fear; insisted it would be safer if we didn't call attention to our meeting at the bank."

"C'mon, I never heard of you opening after hours before."

"I have on rare exceptions. Tonight was one, for a good client and—and friend. Y'see, Neal sold out the Rosebud Hotel tonight."

"Sold the Rosebud!"

Hevis nodded. "To one of his dealers—a Vince Osmond, who'd just hired on in need of a job, new to town with no bankable funds. Made me wonder when he was dickering for the hotel, but turns out his tycoon father paid the tab. Neal was tired of it and glad to sell, but he haggled hard. Both did, cagy as Armenian rug peddlers. Ended up that Vince took the shebang over on the spot for spot cash—twenty thousand dollars."

"Holy—! That's a heap of dinero in one chunk!" the sheriff exclaimed, as a flurry of similar opinions gusted briefly among the four laborers and the spectators who'd overheard. Then the blow died swiftly to a murmuring calm.

Jessie remarked dryly, "Twenty thousand seems to be a rather unlucky number."

"Why . . . that is the amount when it happened, ain't it? Genesee Maddox and now poor Chenault." The sheriff shook his head. "Glad I ain't got no money."

"Coincidence. Seems of late anyone with a deep pocket is apt to fall victim, including an entire train," Hevis countered. His earnestness became more somber as he continued, "Neal didn't want to leave any amount in his safe overnight, not after the attempted robbery. My putting his money in the vault was a simple favor, but he insisted we meet here, refused me or anyone to accompany him from the Rosebud. Saw no reason to risk drawing attention to us, when so few knew he'd the money at all. Well, somebody had an eye on him, obviously, and was waiting when he got here."

"Weren't no money sack on him," the pop-eyed man hastily declared. "Or in the alley, nothin' like it a-tall, I swear!"

"Calm down, nobody's accusing you," the sheriff said. "Now, Charlie—"

"Why don't yuh jus' toss me in the hoosegow," Wolfe said morosely. "You got me all buttered and branded for this'n, and my jawin' won't change—"

"Your loco jawin' won't," Sheriff Beard snapped indignantly. "Now, I want you to tell me straight just how you happened to be here."

Wolfe rubbed his palms on his thighs, raked the brim of his Montana, and said, "It's like this. Around dinnertime, a stranger comes up and says he's a swamper at the Rosebud, and that Mr. Chenault needs to see me about something special. I can't blab, can't pester him, but be sure to meet him at ten-fifteen sharp in front of the bank. I say okay, and the swamper goes off."

"Didn't it strike you as a kinda peculiar request?"

"Nope, can't say it struck me one way or tuther. Y'see, I used to hang around in the Rosebud considerable before—before I had my trouble last year. I knew Mr. Chenault, always figured him for a square shooter, too, so whatever he wanted, that was fine by me as is. I was out front, a coupla minutes early, when I heard a yell. When I ran down in here, I stumbled over Mr. Chenault right where he is. Before I even got a chance to see who it was, these fellers came boiling down. You know the rest."

Before the sheriff could respond, Lucian Hevis cut in irascibly: "That doesn't make a lick of sense, Charlie Wolfe. Neal and I were set to meet here at ten-thirty. It's a few minutes' walk from here to the Rosebud, kinda tight for two meetin's fifteen minutes apart. Course, to figure Neal was planning to make two trips here means on the first trip he planned to leave his money in the Rosebud safe. If you figure Neal doing that, you're a idiot. Or, you can figure Neal planned to make one trip, meet us each separately on time, and take his money along the whole while. If you figure Neal doing that, you're a damn moron. But take your pick. It's your asinine whopper you're stuck with."

The words shook Wolfe; their insinuating charge caused his face to redden, and his fingers to squirm in the palm of his gun hand. Hevis was eyeing Wolfe with accusatory disdain, the surrounding bystanders figuring right along with him, becoming restive and resentful.

Jessie glanced around at the angrily muttering men, and sensed a seething undercurrent building that might explode into mob violence. "Charlie Wolfe may have trouble proving he's innocent," she called, hoping to reason with them, "but not as much trouble as you'll have proving he's guilty. You can't."

"Why, 'cause you don't think he did it?" the pop-eyed man yelled snidely.

"I don't think he did. Maybe you won't when I tell you why." Jessie paused for emphasis, then said, "Where's the money? Neal Chenault doesn't have it, you and your friends don't, and you searched the alley. You got here before Charlie Wolfe could make a break, even if he'd wanted to. And he doesn't have the money on him, either!"

Her hearers stared at her as the significance of her statements sank in.

"Maybe he did have it and threw it away," Hevis suggested.

"If he did, he throwed it up on your bank roof or the saloon's. It sure ain't at either end of the alley; I'll take these guys' word for that," Sheriff Beard declared. "Begins to appear like someone got to Neal before Wolfe did. Whoever it was sure left us a mess to clean up."

There came a disruptive shuffling from up the alley, as the crowd parted deferentially for Doc Terwilliger. Bustling through to the doorway, he grimaced at the body. "We'll have the cussed town so cluttered with corpses somebody'll have to move out to make room," he muttered as he began a swift examination of Chenault. "Wonder who's next?"

"You needn't be looking at me," the pop-eyed man said. "Pick on Anse there. He's lived too long, anyhow."

"I'm younger'n you, you dadgummed stoved-up clodhopper," bawled the insulted one of the three laborers. "You'd be dead right now if yuh wasn't pickled in alcohol."

"I figure they'll have to kill the both of you with a club to get Resurrection Day started," Terwilliger prognosed as he rose and turned to the sheriff. "Damn shame. Chenault got his throat cut; what more can I say?"

"That's enough, thanks." Beard turned to the crowd. "Some of you gents take Chenault to Doc's clinic. And be careful, we don't want his head to fall off." Several men volunteered for reasons known only to themselves, and hoisting the body, they gingerly carted Chenault away up the alley, while the sheriff kept calling, "Break it up! Break it up, now, nothing more here."

Charlie Wolfe watched him, his eyes brightening with hope, and when the sheriff got around his way, he asked, "You don't figure I did it, then?"

"Maybe you did, and maybe not," Beard said non-committally, "For now, get going before I jug you for loitering."

Wolfe drew a deep breath and headed up the alley, squaring his shoulders. The sheriff continued urging others to disperse. The men gradually moved away in twos and threes, men who were saying that the arrest of Charlie Wolfe would put an end to the mayhem around Whitewash, and muttering that sometimes you can't leave justice up to the law.

Jessie headed back to the Rosebud. Outwardly, nothing had altered, the old crew of clerks and barkeeps was there on duty. Business was going as usual. The flaxen-haired dealer and now new boss, Vince Osmond, was presiding over the whole operation from his chair at the poker table, handling the cards and hotel affairs with smooth efficiency. But for her it was not the same Rosebud Hotel.

This one lacked a certain presence that the other Rosebud had. She was going to miss it, and him. Oh, she wasn't anywhere near to donning widow's weeds and shuffling off to some convent; she hadn't been in love with the guy or anything. But she'd found him exhilarating, and full of gumption, and dammit, she'd just plain *liked* Neal Chenault. And that was enough.

Even if the welfare of the territory and the people of Gila Basin had not been concerned, she would have been just as determined. It had become a personal fight now.

Chapter 10

The sun was at its zenith and heat waves were shimmering off rooftops when Ki arrived in town the next day. Stopping at the bank, he deposited the voucher he'd received for the herd in the Slash-C account, then went looking for Jessie.

He found her at the Rosebud, to no surprise, lunching with the delegates in the dining salon. The noontime scene was slow and slack, as usual, but Ki sensed a stewing undertone that almost, and might yet, threaten to erupt with boiling turbulence. Nor was this his first such impression. Already, on way to the hotel, he'd realized that more than midday humdrum was stirring in Whitewash. In the shade of boardwalk overhangs, men grouped in tight, surly clusters. Out the batwing entries of saloons, gutteral mutters spilled from hard talk over hard drink. Yeah, a powwow with Jessie was definitely due.

Unfortunately, she was not alone. She shared a table with two delegates, her bowl of soup, and their full-course meals. One of the delegates was methodically chewing each bite with click-a-clack dentures, while the other was orating, waving his knife for emphasis. Jessie didn't seem to be taking much, if any, notice of the spiel or her soup. She caught Ki's approach, though, glancing up with a tight, perturbed smile and indicating the chair across from her.

Concerned, Ki cut the small talk short and got straight to the point.

"What's the matter is murder," Jessie replied to his question.

"Who now?"

"Neal Chenault." Tersely, her features drawn and strained, Jessie related the brutal mystery. "And there stood Charlie Wolfe," she finished grimly. "Just being there isn't proof he killed Neal, and he didn't have the money or any knife, but he's got a way of looking guilty as sin."

"It's common knowledge he did it," one delegate asserted.

The other nodded. "Word paints him as a ruckus raiser—big drinker and gambler before, now a wringy ex-con on the prod."

"Claptrap and rumors prove nothing," Jessie argued. "Oh, I can't fault anybody. Hurt, scared, robbed, family or friends slain . . . they've good right to be mad. And Neal Chenault, it seems, is the final straw. I'd no idea, but a lot of people cottoned to Neal and were hit hard by his death, by the cruelty. They're riling. And he symbolizes why they're angry. They can focus on him, let him stand for everything, and can concentrate, intensify their rage until . . ." She sighed.

"Maybe not. Plenty more is liable to come out any time, and change their tune," Ki said. "What about this dealer, the new boss?"

"He was seen here the whole time, and I saw him when I came in." Jessie motioned toward the poker table. "The towhead, that's him, Vince Osmond."

An argumentative card game was in progress as Ki turned to look. For a number of deals he continued to watch, long and thoughtfully, measuring Osmond and his play. He was about to turn back when suddenly tempers flared.

A young laborer, more than half drunk, losing a pot he was sure of winning, grabbed the cards and tore them to bits. Osmond spoke to him in tones of quiet remonstrance. The laborer, face flushing with added resentment, started up from his chair while dropping his hand toward his holster. He hadn't reached as far as his shell-belt when Osmond shot out his hand. A small-caliber snub-nosed hideout pistol slid from his sleeve and into his palm. The young laborer ogled the muzzle, Osmond saying nothing, his eyes saying it all. Paling, the laborer sank back in his chair, all the belligerence shocked out of him. Osmond glanced around the table, flicked his pistol back into his sleeve, and began breaking out a deck of fresh cards as if nothing had happened.

"He's smooth 'n' slick as silk," the second delegate commented.

"And cold as a banker's glass eye," Jessie responded.

Ki said nothing. On his face was the expression of a man who is trying hard to call something to mind. Abruptly, his lips quirked in a steely grin and he half rose from his seat. Then he sank back in his seat without a word . . .

A short while later, Doc Terwilliger held an inquest on Chenault. Death by persons unknown, the jury found, plainly believing Charlie Wolfe guilty. While they were there, Ki informed the sheriff of the attempted rustling.

Neal Chenault was buried later that afternoon, following a quick boxing by Fitch, the undertaker. Internment was in the Whitewash Cemetery, the exposed hardscrabble plot lying sun-scalded and glarish. No bird sang in the searing shine; there was no refreshing ripple of water, no comforting rustle of leaf or branch under the caress of a tempering wind. It was in its way as dismal and dreary as the gloom in Perdition Gap.

The wizened desk clerk stood at graveside as if stunned, along with a delegation of hotel staff. The doc and Sheriff Beard stayed at the rear, where the sheriff could watch Charlie Wolfe, who was keeping his distance back at the fringe. An impressive turnout of folks from Whitewash and environs were grouped about, their gazes often shifting covertly from the grave to Wolfe. Obviously one version of what had happened last night had spread around, and it took no wild guess to know who had carried it—Lucian Hevis. Annoyance prickled Jessie as she stood next to Ki, listening to the local preacher intone a eulogy while Chenault was laid to rest.

Like Jessie, Ki kept his expression level and somber, screening the emotions roiling within him. After the service, they remained nearby as the others filed past the gravesite to pay last respects before returning to the task of living. Some of the men, drifting for their horses or wagons, glanced askance at one another, and shot Wolfe looks that promised to kill.

Passing Wolfe, the old desk clerk had a conniption of sorrow and vengeance. "Those murderin' buzzards! We oughta scour these hills and wipe out that masqueradin' gang of renegade sidewinders once 'n' for all!"

"Cut off a snake's head," Hevis sternly declared from closeby, wagging a finger at Wolfe, "and the rest of the varmint won't give you any trouble."

"Easy there, Lucian," the sheriff growled loudly. "I realize how emotional this hour is, and you're het up an' all, but let the law take its course."

Wolfe, who hadn't spoken at all yet, peeled his lips back from his clenched teeth in a mocking grimace. The effect seemed to madden Hevis, who hesitated, scowling. They poised, ready for the break, each determined and wary of the other, locked in a feud of personal animosity.

It was Doc Terwilliger who broke the calldown. Astutely careless and accidental, he blundered into the back of Hevis, his paunch springboarding the banker aside. Before Hevis could recover, Sheriff Beard and a very apologetic doctor were maneuvering him ever so gently toward the horses.

A few more people went on by, and then Jessie invited Wolfe over to graveside for his final respects.

"Ma'am, I'm obliged," he said appreciatively, when they were together. "And for last night, f'sure; I dunno what I'd have done without yuh."

"Counted on Sheriff Beard, and done just fine."

Wolfe was holding his hat in his hand, but the clean, blocked belly nutria Montana he'd worn at the depot was now a trampled, stained hulk. Wolfe wasn't in far different shape from his hat. Dust and dirt matted his clothes, his shirt was ripped, his face bruised and blood-crusted at the lips and nostrils, and one of his glittering devil-may-care eyes had a black beaut of a shiner.

"Yeah, some upset gents don't think much of the law that won't salt me away," Wolfe said, answering Jessie's query. "Leastwise they thought 'nough of the law to not quite kill me."

Casually Ki remarked, "Well, your arm's better, anyway. Did we hear the doc right, that you got bushwhacked?"

"Yep. I was cuttin' at the forks to my place, when I leaned against a passin' bullet. Lead was throwing at a respectable clip, an' I didn't know if there's one or many holed up in the brush, so I split and circled round to my place. Wasn't much of a wound, just a crease, but a bleeder, an' that's what sawbones are for. I tossed the sling next morning. It's scabbing nicely."

139

"What time did it happen?"

"I dunno exact. Two, maybe three hours before midnight."

"Shortly before the raiders hit the Slash-C," Ki reflected, pausing. Then he said amiably, "You oughta stop by the ranch soon. Tonight. Diedre's asking."

Hesitating, Wolfe daubed his nose, saw blood on his sleeve, and responded bitterly: "I don't reckon so. You know how folks will talk."

"Charlie, believe me, the way things are going on her spread, Diedre's in dire need of a man," Ki said, hastily amending, "a good, trustworthy man. Who knows ranching and managing, who can give her a boost, er, hand. I told her this morning, I did, that I figure you're the best lad for the job."

"You did? Do? You really think I'd be up to it?"

"Straight arrow, Charlie. You're a hard man, I'm countin' on it. And I've a feeling Diedre will depend on it often in coming times. Will you try?"

"Well . . . sure, I'll give it a poke. I was gonna go home, and the Slash-C is just a jump away," Wolfe replied gratefully and without an instant's hesitation. "I better get riding, if I'm to see Miss Diedre while it's still agreeable early. Hey, I'll see you tomorrow at the Slash-C!"

Jessie and Ki watched Wolfe hurry in the direction of his horse, and when he was past earshot, Jessie asked, "Ki, are you sure he'll be welcome?"

"Positive. One look at his fight injuries, and Diedre'll melt."

"And patching him up will patch up their old romance?"

Ki shrugged. "I suspect her school and his jail parted them too long, and caused misunderstandings. Or maybe not, and they hate talking in the same room together."

"In any case, you got him out of town without denting his pride. It'll allow tempers to cool, or at least not burn hotter. His ranch could well be a target, too. Thanks, Ki. You didn't have to help Charlie. You didn't have to plan it so he and Diedre could work things out. But you did, and he's safe."

Ki eyed Jessie owlishly. "You don't know the half of it . . ."

Jessie was wrong. In a relatively short time, it became apparent that tempers were not staying the same, much less cooling. They were rising, fast and furious. She should've guessed, Jessie thought, as she watched laborers and ranch hands gathering and growing noisier. These were men of hard action; the blood ran swiftly in their veins, and their passions were elemental. And now, since they couldn't find Charlie Wolfe to vent their rancor on, they had to find some other outlet to relieve their fury. The only one around was Floyd Laslo.

Ki listened to the swelling clamor with disgust. "Did you hear what that guy called Laslo? 'The big scookum he-wolf of the pack!' These guys are talking like your delegates. Now I know they've all gone dipsy-doodle!"

"Since when do mobs operate on logic or sense? They just needed to get stoked on whiskey, then fired to a burning rage by Hevis' tongue-fanning. Now they're goaded up and lynch-talking."

"Sheriff Beard won't stand for it."

"He may not have any choice, Ki. He's alone in the jail—only Nudelman to hold the door, no extra guards on now. We may have to help. Laslo's just a hired hand —certainly no boss. But we need him alive as long as there's any chance he's the weak link of the outfit." She regarded Kit stubbornly. The pride she showed had been a mark of the Starbucks for generations. "We took on this fight when we rode that death-rattler train, and now that Neal is dead, I won't stop—I *cannot* stop—until we finish the fight . . ."

141

* * *

Afternoon eased toward evening, the westering fire
casting scarlet streamers and gilding the distant peaks.
The roving throngs along the shadowed boardwalks
were blurring, but from that murky swarm and the saloons could be heard an increasing tumult of drunken
shouts, harsh curses, and vicious laughter, all filtering
like rising portents.

The lovely blue dusk was sifting down from the hills
like smoky dust when Jessie and Ki repaired to the
Rosebud for a bite to eat. They were midway through
their meal when from outside came sounds of saloons
emptying and boots thumping on boardwalks. They
sprang from their chairs as the mob reached a fever
pitch and descended on the jail.

Up by the law office, the fronting street and boardwalks were black with men. Foremost of the mob was a
big roughscuffer with a sallow face and craggy, over-
hanging brows. He was shouting:

"Toss us the keys, you ol' geezer, and git while you
can!"

Standing before the law-office door, his chair to one
side now, was Deputy Nudelman with his Peabody at
the ready, and a decided quaver to his voice. "I ain't got
'em! Only Sheriff Beard does, and he's a-waiting for
you!"

"Th' devil with the sheriff!" shouted another. "We're
going to string up that murderin' horny toad! You'll tell
us where the keys are after you get a taste of fire on
your feet!"

"None o' that, feller!" cautioned a rangy puncher
nearby. "Nobody's goin' to hurt that ol' jigger. We got
something that'll open the door. C'mon, boys!"

There was a concerted rush. Nudelman managed to
fire his single shot with his shaky hand before they
closed in on him, but the bullet went wild. This made
relief ripple through the siege now; they had been

aware of the destructiveness of the Peabody's .45/70/480 rimfire cartridges. In an instant, Nudelman was disarmed and brushed aside. But a quick search of his person did not reveal the keys.

"Oh, screw 'em," a big man snarled. "Bring that log and get busy!"

Half a dozen men pushed to the front, bearing a heavy beam to use as a battering ram on the door. The big man bellowed out a booming chant, and the rhythm was quickly picked up by the others. The log swung in tempo, its end hitting the door with a thundering crash. The stout barriers creaked and groaned, but withstood their efforts. Again they hurled the beam at it. One of the planks split from top to bottom, and the mob howled its triumph.

"Move off!" Sheriff Beard roared from inside. "Cease and—"

Back had come the beam again, and again it crashed home, drowning out the sheriff's order. Another plank splintered. The door sagged on its loosened hinges.

"Disperse an' go about your business in a lawful manner!" the sheriff yelled out. "You try comin' in, you'll get carried out! I'm nestin' plump, with plenty of shotgun fodder!"

"You ain't gonna torch no shotcannon at us!" the big man blustered with a touch of scorn. "It's ag'in your religion to kill people, Sheriff!"

"The Good Book says, 'I give ye power to tread on serpents and scorpions,'" the sheriff retorted. "So c'mon, you pack o' pizinous rattlers, and feel me do some dead-center treadin'!"

"Give her a good one this time, boys, and it'll do it!" the big man yelled. The battering crew drew back a dozen paces from the door and got set for a running rush. The mob whooped with excitement and anticipation. "Get a good start, now, put your backs into it!"

The exultant whoops changed to yells of alarm as

143

there came a thunder of hoofbeats and a spirited cow-pony bearing the Slash-C brand charged through their ranks, scattering men right and left, bowling others over. With the horse still going full speed, the tall rider leaped from the saddle, landing agilely and rocking back on his heels to keep his balance. Then, bounding forward, he seized the battering ram and tore it away from its holders, balanced its heft once, and then hurled it into the crowd, creating a wild rush to get out of the way. He stepped back, facing the mob.

The rising shout of anger was suddenly stilled as the leaders stared into the black muzzle of a Winchester .44/40 carbine. So far, so good, Ki thought. Jessie had bought the carbines to have long-range weaponry in the wide-open country. But here was the other advantage a big firearm has over, say, a knife. A knife is basic; a carbine carries a menacing quality, even at a distance, and can inspire a hell of a lot of cooperation. Let's hope.

Ki spoke now, and made no speech out of it: "Break it up! Or I will!"

For an instant there was stunned silence. It was shattered by the craggy-browed man's howl of wrath. "Who in hell are you to barge up here and tell folks what to do?"

Instantly the carbine muzzle moved a trifle, until it was lined on the craggy man's broad chest. "This's me. You want an introduction?"

The color drained from the craggy man's face and he seemed to shrivel as he slipped aside from under Ki's point-blank range. But the rest of the mob were coming out of their bewilderment. Voices began to yell:

"What's going on up there!"

"Get going!"

"He's only one man!"

"Kill him!"

Then there was a clatter of hoofs, and Jessie rode to

144

the front, her rented horse plowing another shock wave of tumbling men through the mob. Dismounting at a run, she joined Ki, her carbine grasped firmly, her voice loud and clearly searing with contempt. "Kill me, too! It ought to be easy!"

"What's a dang female clutterin' up here for?"

"Yeah, it ain't decent!"

"Go get away, be quick about it!"

Jessie stood adamantly. "Make me! There're enough of you—a hundred to us two. But don't make a mistake. I'll empty my magazine into you before I go down. Who aims to be first?"

The yells and curses continued, but now they held an uncertain note. It didn't set real right to down a woman, especially a spitfirin' vixen who'd shoot first and God only knew where. Almost unconsciously, men began to edge back.

There was a clunk of latchbolt and a squall of hinges, and the broken door swept open. Sheriff Beard shouldered out in a fuming snit. "I've had enough of this tomfoolery! Why, yuh cowardly, whinin' skunks, pickin' on wimmin! What'll you stoop to next, chillins? If there's a man in sight in one minute, I'll jug him for inciting a riot, and I'll make the pinch stick!"

The front line grew ragged, and the fringes of the mob dissolved as men furtively edged away to make themselves scarce. There was a glimpse of the craggy-browed ruffian ducking out of sight, as the mob continued breaking apart in ever increasing numbers.

"One minute!" the sheriff repeated, brandishing his shotgun. "Move!"

They moved, spreading up and down the boardwalks and vanishing into convenient saloons. In not much more than the sheriff's one-minute deadline, the street in front of the law office was deserted.

Sheriff Beard glared around and finally lowered his shotgun as Nudelmen clumped over, rubbing a bruised arm. Once assured that his deputy was okay, the sheriff turned to Jessie and Ki. "You were damnfool crazy to try it, but it sure came welcome. Another knock and they'd have been through, and a pile of us would've been gone goslings by now. C'mon in." He added as they entered the law office, "But y'know, up till this, I wasn't worried so much of a lynch mob as I was expecting a jailbreak raid."

"I suspect you figured right," Jessie said. "Tonight might've worked out quite differently if the raiders had successfully rustled the Slash-C herd."

"I catch your drift. If Ki reported a swipe, I'd have rode out in pursuit with that mob as my posse. Why, like as not the gang had it planned to strike then and break Laslo out."

Ki nodded, musing, "Out and gone. Somewhere around here they've got to have their hangout, but if it hasn't been found yet, it must be a mighty hidden hole in a mighty small entry."

"Let's check Laslo," the sheriff offered. "I reckon out of plumb gratitude for saving his mangy pelt, he oughta tell us where it is."

It proved close, but not quite. The outlaw was as stubbornly silent as he had been when caught. He gloated that they were wasting their time, sneered he'd never sing and ruin his chances of being sprung, and though he wouldn't say precisely where the hideout was, he did tell them generally where they could go.

Disgusted and frustrated, they returned to the office.

"He won't give," the sheriff grumped, slouching in his desk chair.

"Not as long as he figures to bust free soon," Jessie said.

"He's sworn he'll go in a night or two, ma'am, every coupla days."

"Yes, but what's odd is, I've the impression he genuinely believes it."

Ki was silent, absorbed in thought. Like Jessie, he sensed that the "in a day or two" promise had some sort of buried point to it, maybe a significance, or perhaps a basis, but something more than the empty bluffing of a desperado. Whatever it was, it was in the tone and manner of Laslo's voice, as if he knew there was more brewing. That meant it was more vital than ever to prod Laslo into a confession. Yet normal methods would not work, so . . .

Taking a breath, Ki spoke up. "Maybe we can trick Laslo."

"Trick?" The sheriff frowned quizzically. "I don't follow."

"I have a scheme," Ki said, smiling inscrutably.

Like most good skulduggery, his plot hatched better in darker night when fewer people were about. It was a short delay, just till the first blush of social drinkers were gone, and the hardy nocturnals were rooting in the bars. The town seemed to have calmed down and there was no further talk of lynching, although the general consensus of opinion was that Laslo and Wolfe deserved to be thrown a legal necktie party.

Jessie and Ki passed most of the time at dinner in the Rosebud. Vince Osmond appeared to be running an orderly place, and looked fair to become popular with the customers. The bar was lined three deep and the dance floor was busy, while on a small stage was a trio of bass, banjo and guitar, whomping out spritely tunes. The chuck-a-luck and roulette wheels were clicking, and all the poker tables were occupied, with a high-stakes game at the big table, presided over by Vince Osmond. Kibitzers stood silently watching the game, and Ki joined them for a few moments while Jessie was away. Unobtrusively, he stood almost directly behind the dealer, sufficiently tall to look over the shoulders of men in front of him, and gazed down past Osmond's blond head to the table's card-play.

When Jessie returned, Ki sauntered off to meet her near the barroom entry. Jessie handed him a telegram flimsy, saying, "Great timing. The telegrapher was closing, and'd just got this in from the Circle Star." Ki deciphered the coded message, which consisted of two terse sentences: SUSPECTED OF ARMED ROBBERY AND HOMICIDE IN NEW MEXICO STOP NOTHING PROVED. But the cryptic words seemed eminently satisfactory to Ki, who returned the flimsy to Jessie with thoughtful eyes and a dry, almost sardonic grin steeling his lips.

"The banker Hevis is a little wrong," he said speculatively. "It isn't enough to smash the snake's head, if the body is still wriggling around and inclined to grow a new head. There're brains in this ghost gang, and I've a notion they mightn't all be in one head."

★

Chapter 11

Ki moved stealthily along the rear of the tin-roofed jail, Jessie's custom pistol cocked at the ready in his right hand.

He felt hot and uncomfortable but grimly determined, inside the tight death's-head mask and black, luminously-dyed duster and gloves. They had belonged to the late, unlamented Ghost Raider killed on the road to Slash-C—his sum total estate which Doc Terwilliger had to be cajoled into donating to an unworthy cause. Sheriff Beard threatening to cut off their cribbage matches did the trick, and the doc handed the costume over to Ki, adding dolefully: "You won't have to worry about playin' a convincin' spook, son, if the wrong spectators catch a glimpse. Inside a half-hour you'd catch your death o' a stretched neck or lead poisonin', and be a real spook."

Now, that Ki could believe. He kept a very wary eye out against chance encounters, and hoped none of the respectable citizenry, especially the drunk ones, would catch a passing glimpse of his dancing, spectral movements through the shadows: And he hoped the plan would work. If it didn't . . .

Ki put the thought out of his mind. There was no use anticipating more trouble than already abounded. He made his way as silently as possible toward the barred window at the far end of the adobe-walled building, through which shone a pale light from the lantern on the sheriff's desk inside.

When he reached the window, he keened his ears for some sound from within the cell, but there was none. He reasoned that Laslo was lying on his cot, which was so located as to afford him a view of the window. The outlaw hadn't been asleep minutes earlier, when Sheriff Beard had given Ki the go-ahead. There was no reason to assume that he was sleeping now.

Cautiously raising his head, Ki brought the Colt up in front of him until his eyes and the gun muzzle were on a level with the sill of the barred rectangle. Then he straightened tall, framing the glowing death's-head in the windows and poking the gun through the bars. He made as much noise as he could, just in case Laslo was looking in another direction.

But the outlaw had been lying on his back, gazing up at the window. When he saw the ghostly head and the pistol appear, he cried out in fear and shock and rolled scrambling off the cot. Ki fired twice, purposely aiming wide so that both bullets thudded into the cotton wadding of the cot's mattress.

Laslo was backing against the cell door now, crouching like a cornered animal, his eyes bulging wide with liquid terror. He was screaming for the sheriff in a high-pitched whine, but Beard had conveniently stepped out onto the front stoop, after taking pains to announce he needed a touch of fresh air. He was also preoccupied with the manifold weighty responsibilities of his job, for his normally acute hearing seemingly failed him right then and there.

Ki fired again, missing high by design, although he made it appear as if the shot was hurried due to circumstance. He drew the Colt back then, ducking down and away from the window, racing swiftly along the shadows to the rear of the law office, pulling off his death's-head mask as he ran. He could hear Laslo squalling inside his cell, and it was music to his ears.

When Ki reached the side of the building, Sheriff Beard was there with his revolver in hand. He grinned some around a plug of chaw tobacco, nodded to Ki, and raised his gun arm over his head. He began bellowing his lungs out, squeezing off four shots in rapid succession into the night sky.

By then Ki was over at the mercantile store adjacent to the jail, darting around the back to the unlocked rear door. He slipped through into a small storage area, where he had changed moments before. Shucking it fast, he folded the spectral garb into the duster, black side out, and went to the door, listening.

There was a small but vociferous hubbub outside as those in the vicinity, attracted by the shots, converged on the law office to learn what new scandal was developing. Sheriff Beard insisted it was nothing, nothing a-tall, and told them to cease and disperse. In short order, silence settled beyond the door.

After a moment, there was a soft knock and the sheriff eased through the rear entry. "Nice pottin', Ki. Laslo's still got the screamin' meemies. I reckon maybe your notion may work, if we can get by a stinker of a problem."

"Well, if there's only one. . . . What is it?"

"Wal, Laslo took bad fright. Scairt shitless is close, only his pants are full. Me, I reckon he's got just that many fewer lies he can tell us. You want to go now and brave the consequences, or do we let Laslo stew in his own juices a mite longer?"

"If he's going to talk, it'll be while he's still plenty shaken, fouled, and shamed. We'd best go now."

Leaving, they hastened around front and crossed the street to a saddlery, the shop opposite the law office, where Jessie was waiting. Ki gave her the costume and her pistol tucked in the bundled duster. Then, as she hurried to Doc Terwilliger's, Ki and the sheriff went across to the law office.

Inside, Nudelman was watching Laslo, who stood gripping the bars of his cell with bloodless fists. His face was bone-white in the lantern glare, and his eyes were white orbs, like those of a spooked horse.

Beard frowned sternly. "They got away, Laslo. I'd say you're double-danged lucky you ain't dead twice t'day. Whew! Nobody else is."

"Maybe he won't be so lucky next time," Ki remarked.

"Whatcha mean by that?" Laslo demanded. "Whatcha mean, next time?"

"Your pals trust you not to talk. Trust you dead the most," Ki replied, resting a hip on the sheriff's desk so that he was facing the cell. "They won't stop at two misses, and there's nothing to stop them till they're done."

"They—they wouldn't kill me." Laslo's voice was uncertain, tremulous. "It was, it was just a warning. Yeah—a warning, is all."

"What kind of warning?"

"Whaddya think, saphead? T' keep my trap shut!"

The sheriff snorted. "You're the fool, Laslo—a bigger nincompoop than you look or smell. Maybe yuh can buy a lame excuse like that once, but not twice. That ghost pard of yours pitched three slugs into your cell with you just now. That don't sound like no warning I

152

ever heard of. You ask me, he tried to ventilate your carcass good 'n' proper."

"Crap! I, uh . . . twice? Two misses?"

Ki nodded, casual and calm. "Counting the lynch mob. It was real enough, but afterwards word kept feeding on how it started. Men come up, one here, one there, and tell similar stories that soon form a pattern, Laslo, and yours was simple. A few men in each saloon, whipping up a whirlwind of fast talk and faster drink, loosening it to a howl. Know who the men are, leastwise by sight, and they're your breed of cold-eyed, hard-faced jiggers, long on twist and tight of tie-downs."

"I don't know any sech individuals! Name me one, you name one I know!"

"I'll do better'n that," Ki retorted, thinking fast. "Listen, one guy up front ordered the pack, and I bet you know him. Billy's about your age, big, but sliding to a belly." It was an easy lie to concoct; Billy and those akin of it are dirt-common names, and every bunch has somebody who answers to such descriptions. "He gets too loud when he drinks, and likes to swagger some."

"Him! Bull Pulask— Ne'er mind who, they know I won't talk!"

"They know how to make sure you won't," Beard said coldly. "Or've you got another reason why they'd try to kill you tonight?"

"I—!" Laslo was trying to convince himself that he was hearing lies, that he was in no peril from his pals; his confused conflict showed like a war map on his face. Ki watched fear beginning to win out over whatever loyalties he had, fear and anger at his near-killers. Two! He wasn't that stupid; he knew that disregarding two tries was a dead man's sucker bet.

Finally, he said haltingly, "L-looky here, you gotta protect me. Gotta put a guard outside. If they—"

"We don't have to do nothin' at all," the sheriff retorted. "Far as I'm concerned, your pards can drag yuh off. You ain't no use to us."

"You d-don't mean that!"

"Hell, I don't!"

"But—but you gotta! You're the star-toter!"

Beard snorted and glanced at Ki. "Y'see how they cry law 'n' justice when it's their skin nailed to the outhouse door?"

Ki nodded, eyeing Laslo. "You heard him. Tossing you out will save taxpayer money, too. You help us, we put in a good word at your trial, and maybe you won't dance the hangman's jig. You don't, you're a dead man either way."

Laslo brooded. The jail was very quiet; nobody badgered him as his turmoil continued, his hands clasping and unclasping the iron bars. After several minutes passed, he said in a choked voice, "They deserve whatever happens to 'em! The dirty sidewinders had no call to throw down on me. I ain't no rat, and they knowed it. They had no call!"

"Uh-huh. Wal, yuh wanna tell us about it now?"

"Yeah, Sheriff." Anger had replaced most of his fear now, and his white cheeks were splotched with red. "Yeah, I'll tell yuh some, I reckon. They're some dirty rats that deserve what happens to 'em after what they tried!"

"Aw' ri', start at the top. Who's the big bossman?"

"I dunno, Sheriff, never saw him. Some have—the older crew, a tight clan what don't mix." Laslo paused, and Ki eyed him dubiously and wished the sheriff had led with less of a question. Best to begin small and sink in to the difficult and powerful queries, which get lied about or held close as bargaining chips. Laslo added, "We get our orders written out and left at a drop point out near the cemetery."

"Cem—!" the sheriff bristled. "Sheer flamboozlin' horseshit!"

"God's word, I swear!" A derisive note hit his voice as Laslo challenged: "Go there, see if I'm right and you've the eggs. Supposed to be a big meet of some kind tonight, to divvy the train wreck, I think. It'll be the boneyard."

"What time?" Ki demanded, pulse quickening.

"Midnight."

Beard consulted his pocket watch. "Past eleven now."

Ki nodded, eyeing Laslo. "Talk fast. Where and how do we get there?"

"That big tomb at one end. There's a secret entrance to it, around to the rear. The whole wall slides up, and there's plenty enough room for men an' horses both to pass through."

"So that's it!" the sheriff exclaimed. "Who'd have figured like that?"

"The ol' miner who built it had a passion for secret passages and the like, the way we heard it. When he had the crypt built, he made sure to have that hidden entrance put above it."

Ki frowned on that. "The tomb's too small to keep a dozen horses and men. There must be a passage or two leading underground from inside."

"Yep, like I say, the ol' miner was loony about such stuff. His coffin's on a platform that swings out when you work a hand lever hidden on one side. A ramp goes down into an old mine shaft, plenty wide. Hell, under that area is a maze of passages and shafts. The old miner owned a claim to the area, and had the crypt built on top of all the mine tunneling."

"Wal, is there gold veins in those shafts? Any pro-spectin'?"

"Nary an ounce, Sheriff. Played out a decade ago, plain enough."

"Kilt my idea, too. I figgered the boss don't want the cemetery and tunneling—and the gold—covered by dam floodwaters. It's a good'un; only snag is no gold," Beard grumbled. "Now, Laslo, in this big mine shaft maze, how do we find which one they'll meet in?"

"There's a big grotto at the end of the main shaft under the tomb. Been our bunkhouse for some time, since we hired out of Colorado, when we wasn't pullin' these crazy ghost raids."

Ki asked Laslo where the hidden levers were that opened the tomb entrance and operated the platform leading to the underground ramp. After he and the sheriff got answers on some specific details, they made ready to leave.

"Hey!" Laslo cried out, as they started for the door. "Hey, you're not gonna leave me here alone, are you?"

"No, Deputy Nudelman will sack out here," the sheriff replied.

"This ol' pelican? I'm safer here alone!"

"Swell, be alone," Nudelman retorted, and opened the door.

"Sheriff! Sheriff! You promised me protection!"

"Don't fret, Laslo," Beard snapped over his shoulder. "You'll get everything what's comin' to you." He was last to leave, and from habit, he shut and locked the busted door while Ki and Nudelman waited. He was consulting his pocket watch when Jessie hurried up.

"'Lo, Miz Starbuck. Half past now, Ki. We ain't much time."

"No, not enough to round up a proper posse quietly," Ki allowed.

"What posse?" Jessie asked, mystified. "Why quietly?"

"Laslo jawed like a politico, but didn't know who's his boss," the sheriff explained. "If word got out to the wrong parties, we mightn't find anyone in the graveyard when we get there. Or worse, we might fall into an ambush."

"I see. . . . Graveyard?"

156

But already the sheriff was talking with Ki and Nudelman. "Web here can ride out around to gather all the ranchers and nesters and townsfolk he can locate."

"I'll only tell 'em enough so's they'll join along," Nudelman said.

With that, they checked their weapons and got their horses at the stable, Ki filling in Jessie on the way. Sheriff Beard protested against her going any farther, fearing harm would befall her, that she'd hamper their war-pathing. Preparing to ride with or just behind them, Jessie mounted and waited. The sheriff couldn't wait. Muttering about contrary females, he grudgingly allowed as she could join, but sufferin' spells would be hers alone to deal with.

Under loose rein and busy spur, the three rode out of Whitewash, to what they hoped would be the showdown that would end, once and for all, the ghost killers of Whitewash Cemetery. . .

The graveyard lay quiet; a deep foreboding kind of silence hung like a black pall over the graves. Its stones and wooden crosses stood out of the earth and grasses —and above all loomed the murky pale marble crypt of Jedediah Hargreaves. His tomb seemed to overshadow the rest of the burial grounds, sucking into its core the sounds of the living, making the chirrups of crickets and tree frogs, and even the whisper of a nightbreeze, unheard, unnatural, as if in a vacuum.

In the shadows of some cottonwoods, Sheriff Beard stood, uneasily peering about. Scanning alongside him were Jessie and Ki, both knowing that in spite of their intelligence and common sense, there was an aura present which could not be denied.

They had reached the valley containing the cemetery a short while before, dismounting and walking their hard-run mounts to shelter, both for the horses' sakes and in case guards had been posted. Where they left the horses was out of night eyeshot, but not out of earshot;

but the spindly grove was the best choice of a poor lot. Approaching the cemetery afoot, they circled around until now, downwind of the graveyard, they waited and watched. They had glimpsed the soft glow of a cigar from one of the markers; an indication that a guard was on duty, and that the precautions they had taken were all to the good.

The cigar glowed again, and there was a soft scuffling sound as the guard changed his position. A black figure was spotted, standing and stretching. Then the shadow was gone, melding in with the other obscurations. Ki continued to eye that black patch, affixing it to memory, gauging distance and terrain.

"Cover me," he murmured at last, edging away.

"Come back here!" the sheriff whispered, apoplectic. "You can't—!"

Jessie touched his arm. "Ki can. Anyway, better than we can."

Beard nodded, grudgingly admitting that his lithe days were history, and hunkered down with a Spencer .56-50 rifle aimed in the vicinity of the guard. Jessie scrunched close by with her carbine, ready to kill if Ki were spotted.

Ki slowly, heel-and-toe, inched his way around the perimeter of the cemetery. The glow told him that the guard was facing the trees, and the merest rustling noise, the slightest sweep of grass, would call his attention to Ki. There was one section of bare ground which Ki crawled through, using the cover of the stones as much as possible.

Finally he reached the other side of the crypt from the guard and was able to move a little more freely. The stone of the markers was cold and alien under his fingers as he wound his way through them, feeling his way before stepping down hard, occasionally taking the time to clear the brittle twigs and dry leaves from his path. The guard's silhouette became clearer, the inkiness of his duster costume shades darker than the surrounding black night and gray stones.

Ki was within a half-dozen graves, and then within four, pondering various methods of eliminating the guard as he gradually slithered closer until he could grab him. Past the last one, his hands were stretching for the guard's neck when a branch under his foot suddenly broke with a dry snap.

The slight sound made the guard stiffen and turn, revolver already out and swinging with his movement —squeezing the trigger, Ki saw; and if the guard didn't fire, the sheriff surely would, and either way the alarm would be sounded, warning the others. The guard, tightening his finger, started to yell—

But he never got the chance. Ki, altering his tactics, whipped his left hand out and grasped the man's wrist in an *atemi* hold. The man immediately dropped the weapon from his instantly nerveless grasp. At the same time, the rock-hard heel of Ki's right hand shot forward and smashed the plug-ugly squarely between the eyes. As the unconscious guard started to fall, Ki simply embraced him and moved him away a few feet, to lay him peacefully out of sight behind a boulder. And back there he'd sleep for the next twelve hours, Ki then reported to Sheriff Beard, able to be safely collected by the law.

"Or his pals," the sheriff muttered as they walked back to the crypt. "We're only two—oh, sorry, ma'am, only three—right now, and if we make the wrong move..."

The certain awareness of what would follow a wrong move was left unspoken, though they all knew it would mean at least three more bodies for the ground here.

Outwardly, the large tomb of the rich miner looked impregnable. The marble slabs were fitted tightly; the one huge iron door was corroded and locked, sealed against interest; and not a window was there, barred or not. At the back, where Laslo had told of a secret en-

159

trance, they felt around the smooth stone for the lever that supposedly operated the wall.

Beard marveled, "Woulda loved to seen how they built this . . ."

"Here, I think I found it," Jessie whispered, showing Ki and the sheriff what she was holding. "See here? This carved figure?"

The sheriff studied the column of bas-relief etchings that adorned the support pillars at each corner of the tomb. "Y'mean that miner carved there? The one like on his plaque?" Beard asked, peering closer.

"Yes. His pick is loose; I can move it downward like this. I think that—" Jessie pressed against the pick handle, and from deep inside the pick handle came a soft rumbling, grating noise, like a miniature avalanche.

They all had expected the wall would lift up, just as Laslo had explained, without comprehending the mechanical genius that had designed the secret entrance. Somewhat in awe, they stood back and watched as the complete rear wall slowly tilted on some unseen axis and, without a hesitant motion, rose as one solid piece. At the peak of its arc when the wall was parallel with the earth, there was a sharp click and it stopped.

Ki said, "It'll close in a few seconds, according to Laslo. I'm going inside; you two wait here for the posse."

Now it was Jessie who tried to protest. "No, we can—"

"I'm going to sneak, Jessie, and hide from fights. We don't know what's down there, and could send half the posse to their death if the tunnels and rooms are booby-trapped or well guarded. So spying must be done, but done alone."

With that, Ki handed her his carbine and slipped inside the crypt. And not a moment too soon; the great slab of marble lowered, sealing him inside almost on his heels. The interior was pitch-dark, and he had to feel his

160

way to the bier in the middle of the room. Striking a match, he saw that the crypt was bare, absolutely without any kind of decoration or carving, save for the giant coffin on its stone pedestal. The bier looked as formidable and solid as the crypt itself had seemed, the stone top a full seven by three feet, and six inches thick.

On his second match, he located the hidden lever on the bier that operated its mechanism. He tugged on the lever and then stood back, hands on his daggers in his vest, in case somebody was lurking on the other side. The same near-silent rumbling sound emitted from the tomb, and then it began to swing back on one corner, not halting until it rested against the far wall.

It was like opening a cavern to hell. A wide, stone-hewn ramp led downward from where Ki stood by the bier. The ramp was lost against the rough flooring. With weapons within swift grab, he slowly worked his way down the incline, and when the last of his matches went out, he continued in the dark.

The ramp, wide enough for horses and riders, gently leveled out. Though Ki could not see how high was the tunnel roof, he could tell it was over arm's length. A rider, hunched over his mount, could pass through here, he surmised; and once the passages were lit with fire-brands, the way would be clear for the galloping hordes of Ghost Raiders to come and go quickly. Laslo had been right about this being a mine tunnel, for there had been no attempt at smoothing the sides, and the shoring was still open and bare.

It seemed to Ki to take hours to traverse the black shaft, for he was forced to take as much time here as when he was sneaking up on the guard. The tunnel walls could be sharp; once he cut his palm on a stone edge as he padded along, the passage twisting and turning like an angry riverbed, forcing him to fumble for the sides.

Then, as Ki turned one especially sharp corner, he

saw a faint glow ahead, like the mingling of fireflies. He stepped faster, now having a guiding point, and as he drew nearer, the wavering sparks began to take form. When they were steadier and brighter, he knew that he was entering the den of the ghost gang. He heard the first low murmurs of voices, and occasional crude guffaws and rank, sharp swearing. He edged closer, his eyes on the scintillation before him. Rounding another wide curve, he backed against the wall and pressed close to the gloom, unmoving, almost not breathing.

Just ahead was a large grotto, a hollowed-out room about fifty feet square—if it had been square. Two lanterns were in niches along the walls, their glow adding to the radiance of the ghost-costumed men, who were grouped around a conference-sized table in the middle of the floor. Ki counted eleven raiders there. Heading the table was a spectre draped in a white hood and duster. Ki couldn't identify the man by only two eyeholes and hands resting on the table; but realized that that had to be the boss, to get away with that outfit.

Around the grotto were crates and barrels of supplies, and on the table were khaki canvas bags with the territorial seal. They were, Ki figured, the emptied sacks of Blue River dam money stolen from the train. Taken as a whole, the grotto was giving Ki what the Circle Star crew called a blister—angry red, burning and smarting. He'd've liked the grotto taken as a whole, in fact, and it might become a fact if the posse arrived in time. Hell, for all he knew, the posse had already arrived, and everyone was waiting for him. Figuring it was time to start back, Ki eased back away from the grotto—

—And eased back into the cold, dull muzzle of a large-bore gun.

★

Chapter 12

"Damn handy of yuh, stranger," rasped the gruff voice of an unseen man, his pistol digging Ki in the back. "Be hard to miss much like this. Now, walk!"

Ki walked, inwardly cussing himself for not having caught onto the man's presence. Didn't happen often, and rarely this blankly; it was as though the man had simply materialized with a revolver stuck in his spine, and Ki never did find out any different. Wasn't crucial anyway, compared to being prodded out in full view of the now alerted raiders. He half expected lead to come shattering through him right then and there, but instead the outlaws seemed bent on talking him to death, all shouting at once, the racket reverberating around the grotto as he was nudged on toward the table.

The white-robed wonder was loudest of all. *"Quiet!"* he shouted. After the outlaws had toned down, he told the man behind Ki, "Take his gun."

"Don't carry any," Ki spoke up, gingerly opening his vest to prove his point. He thought he recognized the voice of the leader, but he knew who it was, he and Jessie having figured it out a spell back. "Evening, Hevis. Taking more night deposits?"

The white-robed man was silent for a beat. Then he said exasperatedly, "So you recognized my voice, eh? Well, why'd you hafta go blabber it for? If I'd wished them to know, I wouldn't have this on, you dolt!" Lucian Hevis reached up and removed the white hood, amid murmurs from the assembled outlaws. "You ruined that. But finding our secret little hideaway will be your ruin." He brought up a Colt .41 Frontier revolver and thrust it under Ki's nose. "And I think I'll attend to that delight myself. Now, how'd you find out about here?"

Ki shrugged. "Don't recall. Newspaper article, maybe."

"Laslo, I betcha!" a raider snapped out. "Knew he'd rat on us!"

Hevis nodded, eyeing Ki. "Who else knows? Who came with you?"

"Rode out myself. But Beard knows, and is out rounding up a posse right now," Ki replied, wanting Hevis to know his hideout was known, but not to know anyone was hiding out above. "They'll be here within the hour."

"I couldn't do better if I'd planned it," Hevis said, with a wintry smile. "We'll be gone within ten minutes. By the time the posse gets here, there won't be a trace of us. The money off the train has been divvied, and soon's the boys finish their last little job, they'll be riding on. And the posse will be out here snufflin' about, not botherin' us."

"What's the new job—blowing up the dam?" Ki asked sarcastically.

"Why, yes. Bury the construction area under rock and debris that'll take six months to clear away. By then I'll be one of the wealthiest men in this region, because the region will still want the dam built, despite the delay. Wouldn't mind dabbling in politics. How's Governor Lucian Hevis sound to you?"

Repressing a shudder, Ki worked on stalling as long as possible, to give the posse time to reach the cemetery. "How d'you reckon you can get so rich, Hevis? What's behind the raids and the sabotage of the dam project?"

"It won't work, y'know. Now, over to that side, that's where we're going."

"But I don't know, Hevis. I never learned business."

"Well, then, I'll tell you as we go. I don't want to bloody up here, but I will if you balk. March!" Gesturing with the revolver, Hevis fell in behind as Ki headed across the grotto. "The Southeastern Cattleman's Exchange and Trust Bank owns the mortgages of the property of ninety percent of the small landowners in the Gila Basin. The construction of the dam will enable them to pay off their mortgages, to prosper, the land hereabouts productive and fertile with proper water control. The Gila Basin will be worth a fortune when the dam's built!"

"So by stopping the project for six months to a year, you hope to drive the settlers off their land," Ki asserted, coming to the side of the grotto. The light was soft, like summery twilight, the lantern niches chancing to be placed where their illumination cast well on this side. The immediate area was taken up by a hodgepodge intersection of tunnels and shafts, now in an abandoned, crumbling shambles after decades of neglect and erosion. Ki, glancing about, continued to talk to Hevis: "You'll foreclose on their mortgages, and then buy up the property at next to nothing under a series of phony names."

"Precisely. And you know nothing about business." Hevis' words were mocking. "It's been working. The ghost raids have everyone frightened, and most small owners are hanging on the hope of the dam's imminent completion. A handful have already defaulted, moving out, and the rest won't last out a year without the dam. Before construction begins at long last, I'll have refused them extensions on their loans, and foreclosed. When the dam is finally completed, I'll own a large percentage of the Basin. Go left now—go on."

Leftward bored the mouth of a tunnel and the open pit of a shaft. Beyond the junction with the shaft, the tunnel ran only a few yards before totally blocked by a cave-in, with rocks and beam fragments and other debris profuse along its entire length. Ki could not see down into the shaft—though his hunch was that Hevis planned to give him that chance close up—but even from this distance, it was evident that the shaft suffered the same state of collapse and decay.

"What about the large landowners?" he asked, peering ahead, the grotto lantern-light fading rapidly. "The big ranchers won't be driven out by a delay in the dam's construction. You know they don't want the dam at all."

"So? They're big 'cause they're smart, and smart folk are less obstinate and less resistant to the right kind of pressure. And I may be a big rancher by then, too. Hard for a lady to lose family and kin, left with a big ranch responsibility, not to lean on her banker for aid and comfort."

A narrow path of sorts seemed to thread into dim obscurity, one side hemmed in by rubbled mine walls, the other side skirting the black abyss of the mine shaft. The time for stalling was over, Ki knew. Even though the posse hadn't arrived yet, he'd have to make his move fast, before he got to the shaft.

"No Charlie Wolfe to louse up the action, I take it?" As he asked, Ki stumbled and hesitated, as though confused, and bumped against Hevis.

Hevis was answering "That rogue is bound for a bad fate" when he was jostled by Ki, and impatiently he stabbed Ki with his revolver, adding, "You, you're taking your hell-bound fate—"

The rest was lost in the echoing report of his revolver. By then it was not jabbing into Ki's side; Ki had arched his spine so that the thrusting barrel slid from the small of his back, while he pivoted with his left arm to deflect the barrel away. Hevis was wobbling, arms wavering, and managed to loosen a shot the one instant it might do serious damage. Ki felt the shock wave of its exploding gunpowder, and the snap of the bullet as it passed his ear. And then he had hold of Hevis, shoving the man backwards, his hand slashing downward in a disarming chop. The Colt revolver dropped, skittering aside.

But the path alongside the shaft hole was very narrow, and slippery with loose gravel and pebbles. Hevis, feeling himself slip on the gravel, didn't fight back in accustomed style. He grabbed Ki in a kind of angry frenzy, to balance himself, clawing with unusually long fingernails and kicking frantically.

Ki found himself battling less a man than a mauling animal. Sinewy fingers scratched and pummeled his head and torso, while Hevis smashed at him with his pistol, battering his neck and upper back. He levered against the rock wall, and tried to swing Hevis away, but the man only panicked worse, grasping Ki's throat with as many fingers as he could manage, and clinging for dear life, strangling Ki to death.

Ki felt one of his feet sliding off the edge. He wavered, having to compensate for himself and the man who was glued to him. He regained his foothold and tore his throat free of Hevis' throttling squeeze, then jackknifed his body forward, his shoulder striking Hevis midway between his ankles and his knees. Hevis hinged, folding over him like a sack of feed, and before the banker could recover and latch onto him again, Ki rolled away and stopped at the very brink of the shaft.

167

Hevis vaulted over him, and a wailing cry of terror echoed up through the cavity, receding hollowly into the shaft's black depths. There was a soft, distant thump of meat striking rock, and then silence.

Gasping, Ki rose and leaned against the rock wall to catch his breath. Voices rising in concern over Hevis were rippling through the grotto, making it abundantly clear that at any moment they would come to check. Quickly retrieving the dropped .41 Colt, Ki hurried back the short distance to the grotto, the only way he knew to get out. With one down and eleven to go.

That old element of surprise helped. Ki tore into the grotto and actually got rather far, considering, before the startled outlaws dove scrambling for their weapons. Jumping back, Ki fired Hevis' revolver with deadly, swift accuracy. There were two almost instantaneous explosions of glass as Ki's bullets sent the two lanterns in the grotto spinning out of their niches to shatter on the floor.

The cavern was suddenly plunged into complete darkness, save for the ghostly luminosity of the clothing worn by the outlaws. As they burst into an uproar of confused shouts and curses, Ki raced for the passage he had taken from the crypt. He tried to remember its twists and turns in the utter black, and was only partially successful, gashing his clothes and flesh as he tried too quickly to feel his way along the walls.

He could hear scurrying noises behind him, growing louder as they gradually gained on him. His head start was dwindling to a matter of seconds, and if the bier platform above had been closed by the outlaw who'd captured him, he was good as done for; he had no idea where the lever to operate the platform was located on this side. Glancing back often, he finally saw the flickering glow of the pursuing raiders, and bracing himself with feet wide, triggered two bullets down the passageway just as two of the spectral figures loomed into view.

Onc of them half turned, with lead high in his chest, and crumpled to the floor. The other snapped a wild shot at Ki while hurriedly retreating.

Ki spun around and began running upward again. His guiding hands on the side wall were being cut and scraped in a dozen more places by the sharp edges of rock. To his relief, he found as he neared the ramp that the platform was still swiveled wide. There was just enough grayness in the black to indicate the opening in the crypt. He reached the ramp and sprinted up it, gaining the cold stone floor of the tomb.

Without stopping, Ki went pawing for the lever to swing the platform closed. Gasping, he jerked it up. The platform rumbled and began to swivel shut—and none too soon. Skeletal dancing light illuminated the ramp Ki had just climbed, the raiders heaving into view in the passage below. A salvo of shots, all missing badly, echoed in the confined space, drowning their cursing invectives to stop the sonofabitch.

The sonofabitch was already racing across the blackened crypt before the platform had fully closed. Furiously, he felt along the entrance wall, seeking the lever that would open it from the inside, damning himself for not having pumped the information from Laslo when he'd had the chance.

Precious seconds ticked by. Sweat beaded his forehead as he glanced over his shoulder and saw the platform start to swing open again. The raiders had activated the gizmo from the passageway below. Feverishly, his bleeding fingers moved over every inch of the smooth marble of the wall—and then, just when it seemed too late, he touched the lever. It was located in a small recess in the stone, almost at floor level. Ki wrenched it sharply downward, and immediately the entire wall began to slide up.

Ki waited only long enough for space enough at the bottom. Then he rolled flat and squeezed under the wall, out into the softer black of night, and launched running for the nearest gravestone that could afford him cover. The wall was all the way up now, and the outlaws were charging across the crypt from the open platform, firing at his back.

Diving headlong at one of the wide granite markers, Ki twisted in behind the protective stone as more shots echoed behind him. There was no other sound, no sign of Jessie and Sheriff Beard, much less a posse— Where were they, Ki thought frantically, what in hell had happened to them out here? The outlaws were pouring from the tomb, fanning to encircle him beyond effective range of his throwing weapons, leaving him the two or fewer bullets remaining in Hevis' revolver . . .

Suddenly, from the surrounding darkness, burst a volley of other shots, followed by a coldly shouted, authoritative command. "Drop your irons!" thundered the voice of Sheriff Beard. "Drop 'em and give up, else we'll cut you down where you stand! You're all arrested!"

Shocked confusion ripped among the outlaws. Several of them opened fire, pitching lead in the direction of the voice, and then all hell broke loose. The night erupted in brilliant muzzle flashes. Four of the outlaws fell instantly, wounded or dead. Others scurried for the tomb, trying to open the wall, which had already slid closed again, and were downed by the relentless fire. The remainder slung their weapons and threw up their hands, clustering in a small circle of surrender and bawling for mercy.

Ki rose from behind the gravestone, seeing Jessie and the sheriff materialize out of the night, while two dozen possemen began appearing from their concealment around the cemetery. They kept their weapons trained as Sheriff Beard passed behind the outlaw group, securing hardware and snapping on cuffs.

"Sorry we didn't hit 'em sooner," the sheriff told Ki,

when the last of the Ghost Raiders was cuffed. "But it happened kinda fast, and we didn't know if it was you or not, rollin' out like that."

Ki grinned wearily. "Worked out fine; you corraled the pack."

Jessie looked disappointed. "I hoped we'd catch Hevis red-handed."

"Oh, I ran into Hevis," Ki assured her. "He's down there."

"Jessie told me what yuh figured," Beard said, scowling. "I never did much cotton to Hevis. Too eager, too danged pushy."

"He pushed himself off into a mine shaft. Here, this is his gun."

"Don't that beat all?" Taking the gun from Ki, Beard added, "I reckon that does make it about all, don't it?"

Shaking her head, Jessie turned to the posse. "The sheriff wants you to take charge of this bunch and herd them to jail. Don't take any chances; shoot to kill if they try a break," she yelled. Then she said to the startled sheriff, "You come with us, we're in for some fast riding. And I've a hunch you'll do yourself a big favor, if you'll do a small one for me . . ."

Whitewash had about roared itself out. The few remaining lights were being dimmed, the last of the saloons emptying as tired drunks sought sleep. Little knots of revelers skalleyhooted out of town, potshotting holes in the night sky.

There were still some diehard drinkers and gamesters in the big Rosebud. Weary bartenders polished glasses. The band had packed in and the hostesses were sitting around, rubbing aching feet. Vince Osmond sat at the big poker table and shuffled cards for a final few hands.

Abruptly the entrance door flew open and three figures stepped inside, heading directly for the poker table. Jessie looked stern, her eyes as coldly green as arctic waters. Flanking her on either side were Sheriff Beard and Ki, expressions bleak as chiseled granite. Groups from lobby to barroom stared and fell hushed, and Osmond laid the card deck aside, tense and watchful, as the trio came to his table.

The sheriff's voice rang out, edged with steel: "Genesee Anders, alias Genesee Maddox, you're hereby charged with robbery and murder. Anythin' you may say—"

At the sound of those names, the dealer surged erect. His right hand shot out like the head of a striking snake, his stubby hideout gun snapping against his palm. But even as he was pulling the trigger, he reeled back and fell with a crash, taking chair and cards with him, his right shoulder drilled by a bullet.

Keeping her pistol trained for a second shot, Jessie peered through the powder smoke with a certain satisfaction. The dealer lay writhing and moaning, the gun he had drawn on the floor beside him. Ki and the sheriff glanced quickly around the room, deciding there was nothing to be feared from the stunned gathering, and the sheriff went over for a look at the dealer.

"Fetch the doc," he called out, then glanced up at Jessie. "Wal, I did what you asked, and it sure made him uncork. But dang it, this feller can't be Maddox. I recollect Genesee well, an' he had black whiskers and hair."

Jessie smiled. "Whiskers can be shaved off. And take a good look at the roots of his hair."

The sheriff obeyed, exclaiming, "Why, it shows black!"

"That's right. He bleached his black hair to disguise himself."

"That don't make him dead. An' I saw Genesee dead, or his bones, anyhow."

Ki spoke up. "Not his, Sheriff. Those're the bones of the old Slash-C cook, Lok Yuan. Genesee was gone when the ranch house was torched, leaving Lok Yuan's body downstairs so that the remains would be mistaken for his. Genesee and his Ghost Raiders had killed Lok Yuan a while before, and Genesee spread word that the cook had quit and left."

"Now, hold on! Whaddyuh mean, *his* Ghost Raiders? Did we or didn't we just round up that gang, with Lucian Hevis there as boss?"

"Yeah, but Hevis was like a junior partner. Genesee was the head of the original gang, here and in New Mexico, where they operated under a different name." Glancing up, Ki added, "Good, here comes the doc. I'll want him to corroborate something I'll have to say."

While Doc Terwilliger treated the blaspheming dealer's wound, Sheriff Beard continued to press Jessie and Ki for explanations.

"You two got me discombobulated and in sore need of a drink. Now, what makes you reckon t'was Lok Yuan and not Genesee got burnt to bones?"

Ki answered, "The skull I found. We'd no reason then to suspect Genesee of anything, but it started us to wonder. He hadn't been seen leaving, his bedroom door was locked, and only the bones of one skeleton were in the ruins."

"That sums up Genesee. Why'd you think the skull wasn't his?"

"Because, Sheriff, I knew it wasn't the skull of a Caucasian, as Genesee undoubtedly was. There's a visible difference between the skull of a Caucasian and a Chinese, which isn't hard to catch after seeing some of both."

"That's right," Doc Terwilliger confirmed. "Just a limited knowledge of comparative anatomy is needed to recognize that difference. I missed it, I hate to admit, but bring me back the skull, and I'll prove it by measurements."

"The only Chinese we heard about was Lok Yuan,

but he shouldn't have been there, either," Jessie said. "A cook doesn't hang around in the boss's room late at night, so he must've been downstairs and likely dead, or he'd have fled the fire. But Jingo Paloo told us Lok Yuan quit two days before, so why'd he be back in the ranch house if he hadn't been brought back, and if brought back, odds were he was brought dead. Proof of that came later, with this." Jessie took out the little silver rod with a knob at one end. "Remember this?"

"Sure, that's the dofunny I found on one of Laslo's Ghost Raider pards," the sheriff said, studying the rod again. "Still dunno what it is."

"It's a chopstick. The Chinese use them to eat with instead of forks. The raider must've stole it off Lok Yuan's body," Ki asserted. "Now, y'see, pieces were fitting together. We figured Lok Yuan was killed by the raiders, and the body was in the fire. Genesee didn't show up later with any excuse. His supposedly robbed safe had its combination knob and tumblers intact, so it must've been left unlocked or opened by combination, not smashed or blown open as you'd expect under the circumstances. It sure looked like Genesee was mixed up with the Ghost Raiders, so we began working on that angle."

"But why'd he do it? Why go to all that trouble to stage his death?"

"Things had come to a head," Jessie told the sheriff. "For one, he knew sooner or later his past would catch up. He claimed to've been from Texas, but crooks often name some area near where they're from, and actually he'd operated with a gang in New Mexico. He never quite got caught, though he was suspected of robbery and murder, and when New Mexico got too hot, he moved here. He wasn't Maddox blood kin, just a grandfather's stepson, and readily killed Caleb Maddox to gain the Slash-C as a base for his outfit. That changed, of course, when he teamed with Hevis, and he had to go hire a new regular crew. But now Diedre was coming home, posing a threat to his control and secrecy."

"Ironically, she already suspected him, but as a pawn of the anti-dam big ranchers. No doubt he was milking information out of them to plan his raids," Ki added. "In any case, he couldn't simply kill Diedre, because of Hevis."

Beard nodded. "Yeah, Hevis sure tangled his twine over that gal."

"And that brought Genesee a third complication," Jessie continued, "by name of Charlie Wolfe. They probably never got along, and Wolfe coming round to spark Diedre was a pesky risk he didn't need. Also, Wolfe's spread was too close and in the way, we figure. Either Genesee or his raiders shot at him en route to their hideout after the Slash-C fire. And Hevis hated Wolfe, who'd the inside track with Diedre, and he must've pestered Genesee something fierce to get rid of him. So Genesee framed Wolfe, but Wolfe returned from jail a lot sooner than expected, and the whole wrangle started over. So when the chance arose, he and Hevis framed Wolfe again, framed him good."

"Still, Genesee might not've played dead if it wasn't for Hevis," Ki said. "We don't know exactly when or how they joined together, nor why, until tonight. Each had what the other needed. Genesee had the force and Hevis had the power to pull off a massive land grab after a series of lootings. Before Hevis spilled the reason, we'd already decided Genesee must be cahooting with someone familiar with the area—so familiar, as it turns out, he knew about the secret of Jedediah Hargreaves' tomb."

"I get it now," Beard said. "Hevis was assistant manager, a glorified teller, at the bank, back in the boom days when the miner was alive. Why, he might've handled some of Hargreaves' financing o' his tomb, with Hargreaves swearing him to secrecy."

Jessie nodded. "Likely so. There're others who've lived around here a long time, though, and we couldn't narrow it to Hevis on that alone. The paint on the Ghost Raider costumes proved the key. It's a luminous paint that shines in the dark, not something you can buy in the average town. You have to send away for it, and folks in places like this usually send to one of the big mail-order houses when they want something not available at home. So I had my office check into that, and it was learned that a shipment of luminous paint was shipped to Lucian Hevis. That's where he slipped bad."

"From what Hevis told me down in the grotto," Ki said, "the gang was disbanding tonight after destroying the dam. That would've taken Genesee's say-so, which he gave, seeing it as a good time to retire as Genesee Maddox. So he sold that big herd to Ephram Zephyr and then had his men rustle it. He got away with the herd and the twenty thousand dollars Zephyr paid for it as well. And he arranged it to appear that he died in the ranch house fire, so he could stay on unsuspected, keeping tabs on Hevis and eventually reaping his share of the land grab."

"And he came mighty nigh gettin' away with it, too," Sheriff Beard muttered. "How'd you tumble to Vince Osmond bein' Genesee?"

"Well, once we decided Genesee was pretending to be dead, we figured that if he hung around, he'd be in disguise. Genesee wore whiskers and had black hair, so we looked for clean-shaven men with different-colored hair," Jessie explained. "Then Vince Osmond happened along and was hired as dealer. Right there we had something to go on. Neal Chenault had mentioned that Genesee was good at cards, so good in fact, that he once jokingly offered him a job dealing. Genesee remembered that when he needed an excuse to stick around."

"To get the job, he murdered Emile Gothe," Ki said. "Remember, Sheriff, the startled look on Gothe's dead face? Gothe disappeared the night before the ranch house fire. He knew Genesee, of course, and when he found Genesee in his room, he was surprised, not scared. He never had a chance, any more than Chenault had. Chenault was killed by a knife, too.''

"That was another angle that tied up," Jessie said. "Also, when we tried to get a line on Genesee, as Maddox, in Texas or new Mexico, there was nothing to be learned about a man answering his description. But when I sent along Vince Osmond's description, it was different. I'd already decided that Osmond had shaved off a heavy full beard very recently.''

Sheriff Beard frowned in perplexity. "How was that, ma'am?"

"See for yourself. Osmond, or Genesee, has pale cheeks and chin, but he's tanned around his eyes and upper cheekbones. He probably grew the beard to cover his knife scar, which now helped to distract attention. Then Ki managed to get a close look at his hair. He'd neglected to keep bleaching, and down at the roots a trace of black was showing as his hair grew out.''

Ki sighed. "That about cinched it, but too late to save Chenault. He'd sold the Rosebud for the exact amount lifted from the Slash-C safe—a helluva big coincidence —and then was sent to his death by Genesee and Hevis, murdered by one of the gang. And Wolfe was lured to the scene just at the right time to take the blame for it.''

"As sure as we were, we couldn't prove anything conclusively, and we still didn't know how to catch the Ghost Raider gang itself. I imagine if we hadn't got the breaks with Laslo, things might've worked out differently.''

"Miz Starbuck, you might call it the breaks, but I got another name for it," the sheriff declared with frank admiration. "What you dug up and Laslo's confession will be plenty 'nuff to convict the whole stinkin' kaboodle of 'em. And Genesee here can fill in the cracks, if there are any that need fillin'."

"Th' hell!" Genesee snarled painfully through gritting teeth. "You blundering arsehole, if it weren't for these two meddlers, we'd have succeeded. You'd never have caught us, never!"

Sheriff Beard grinned. "P'raps, p'raps not. But you're caught now, ain't yuh, Genesee? And that's all that matters."

Jessie and Ki smiled in accord. They had the feeling that everything was going to work out just fine from now on. The territorial money would be recovered in short order, the construction of the Blue River dam would soon begin, and there would be no more terrorism from Genesee Maddox and his Ghost Raiders of Whitewash Cemetery.

★

Chapter 13

The ceremony was held in the morning, before the heat of the day wilted the festivities.

The sun was just over the top of the mountains, a yellow blaze in a light blue setting, making the waters of the Blue River sparkle and shimmer. A large throng was gathered at its banks, talking and laughing above the monotonous roar of the cascades below, the Blue having eaten a deep gorge in the bedrock, a gorge that would serve as the sides to the new dam.

Most of the people at the ceremony were of the Gila area, both the mountain country and the Basin. Rarely was there any kind of entertainment of such caliber in their lives, and they made sure that they attended, even if it meant a day's journey or more. Ah yes, and the delegates were on hand, along with a delegation of construction project executives headed by one Ebenezer Toomey.

At the exact point of new construction, a large wooden parade platform had been erected and gaily decorated with red-white-and-blue bunting. Several dozen folding chairs had been set up on the platform, behind a speaker's podium, to seat the delegates and dignitaries.

As Ebenezer Toomey remarked to Jessie, beside whom he was sitting as they waited for the official presentations to begin, "If'n they could've found a brass band somewhere around these parts, that'd be here too."

Jessie laughed appreciatively. The elderly, rotund man was rather a flirt, but in a harmless fashion. "Just an old dog who's long lost his teeth." Toomey had not lost his humor, smarts, or memory, however, and at one point piqued her interest by recalling the old boom times in Whitewash.

"Yep, I recollect when Jedediah Hargreaves built his tomb—just afore the gold began to poop out around here. But then, ol' Jed was always one to time things right. He got sick, knew he was going to die soon, so he sent all the way to St. Louis for the marble and workmen. Wouldn't have any local labor on it; kept everything a big secret. At the time, nobody knew why. Now we do."

"Seems quite odd to me why a dying man would go to such lengths," Jessie remarked. "He wouldn't be around to reap the rewards."

"Ol' Jed was a strange 'un," Toomey explained. "Always talking about being buried alive, on account of a mining accident when he was a button. He was caught in a cave-in for five days, I heard tell, with eight others. He was the lone survivor. I guess that can change a man some."

"So he was afraid of having it done to him again," Jessie replied. "And I bet he filled those tunnels with food and water and made sure it was a secret so others wouldn't steal from him."

"I'd hazard so, ma'am. A far worse fate happened to it, which got caught in time, thanks to you."

"Well, I'm just glad things worked out okay." Jessie

looked out over the crowd, then commented, "Lots of things turned out nicely, I'd say. Look yonder, at Charlie Wolfe."

"Where?" Toomey asked, then said with a grin, "Oh, over by the water barrel. Say, he wound up with a tasty prize for his grief. If the young filly he's squiring ain't a fine morsel, I've lost my eyesight."

"You're ogling well, sir. I understand they're going to be married before too long, and've asked Ki to be best man at the wedding."

"Yikes! Excuse me, but I know a kindred spirit when I meets one, and Ki at a weddin' is like puttin' a fox in the hencoop."

It was along toward eleven before the festivities finally got under way, and they lasted for more than two hours, mainly because some of the chosen speakers tried to rival the hot, arid wind that blew over the dam site. But it was a fine program, and when the delegates presented a check representing the one hundred and fifty thousand dollars to Ebenezer Toomey, the large audience clapped and carried on for a fair ten minutes.

As she listened to the cheering, Jessie thought it was odd, the way people were—superstitious and childish and frightened by a new innovation one day, they could execute a complete reversal the next. But in this case, she couldn't fault them at all, not with the erection of the Blue River dam meaning so much to the development of the American Southwest.

Watch for

**LONE STAR AND THE
MONTANA LAND GRAB**

sixty-fourth novel in the exciting
LONE STAR
series from Jove

coming in December!

☆ From the Creators of **LONGARM** ☆

The Wild West will never be the same!

LONE STAR

LONE STAR features the extraordinary and beautiful Jessica Starbuck and her loyal half-American half-Japanese martial arts sidekick, Ki.

_LONE STAR AND THE GUNPOWDER CURE #47   0-515-08608-8/$2.50
_LONE STAR AND THE LAND BARONS #48   0-515-08649-5/$2.50
_LONE STAR AND THE GULF PIRATES #49   0-515-08676-2/$2.75
_LONE STAR AND THE INDIAN REBELLION #50   0-515-08716-5/$2.75
_LONE STAR AND THE NEVADA MUSTANGS #51   0-515-08755-6/$2.75
_LONE STAR AND THE CON MAN'S RANSOM #52   0-515-08797-1/$2.75
_LONE STAR AND THE STAGECOACH WAR #53   0-515-08839-0/$2.75
_LONE STAR AND THE TWO GUN KID #54   0-515-08884-6/$2.75
_LONE STAR AND THE SIERRA SWINDLERS #55   0-515-08908-7/$2.75
_LONE STAR IN THE BIG HORN MOUNTAINS #56   0-515-08935-4/$2.75
_LONE STAR AND THE DEATH TRAIN #57   0-515-08960-5/$2.75
_LONE STAR AND THE RUSTLER'S AMBUSH #58   0-515-09008-5/$2.75
_LONE STAR AND THE TONG'S REVENGE #59   0-515-09057-3/$2.75
_LONE STAR AND THE OUTLAW POSSE #60   0-515-09114-6/$2.75
_LONE STAR AND THE SKY WARRIORS #61   0-515-09170-7/$2.75
_LONE STAR IN A RANGE WAR #62   0-515-09216-9/$2.75
_LONE STAR AND THE PHANTOM GUNMEN #63   0-515-09257-6/$2.75
_LONE STAR AND THE MONTANA LAND GRAB #64   0-515-09328-9/$2.75
_LONE STAR AND THE JAMES GANG'S LOOT #65   0-515-09379-3/$2.75
(on sale January '88)
_LONE STAR AND THE MASTER OF DEATH #66   0-515-09446-3/$2.75
(on sale February '88)

Please send the titles I've checked above. Mail orders to:

BERKLEY PUBLISHING GROUP
390 Murray Hill Pkwy., Dept. B
East Rutherford, NJ 07073

NAME_____

ADDRESS_____

CITY_____

STATE_____ZIP_____

Please allow 6 weeks for delivery.
Prices are subject to change without notice.

POSTAGE & HANDLING:
$1.00 for one book, $.25 for each
additional. Do not exceed $3.50.

BOOK TOTAL $_____

SHIPPING & HANDLING $_____

APPLICABLE SALES TAX $_____
(CA, NJ, NY, PA)

TOTAL AMOUNT DUE $_____

PAYABLE IN US FUNDS.
(No cash orders accepted.)

LONGARM

Explore the exciting Old West with one of the men who made it wild!

__0-515-08607-X	LONGARM AND THE GREAT CATTLE KILL #91	$2.50
__0-515-08675-4	LONGARM ON THE SIWASH TRAIL #93	$2.75
__0-515-08754-8	LONGARM AND THE ESCAPE ARTIST #95	$2.75
__0-515-08796-3	LONGARM AND THE BONE SKINNERS #96	$2.75
__0-515-08838-2	LONGARM AND THE MEXICAN LINE-UP #97	$2.75
__0-515-08883-8	LONGARM AND THE TRAIL DRIVE SHAM #98	$2.75
__0-515-08907-9	LONGARM AND THE DESERT SPIRITS #99	$2.75
__0-515-08934-6	LONGARM ON DEATH MOUNTAIN #100	$2.75
__0-515-08959-1	LONGARM AND THE COTTONWOOD CURSE #101	$2.75
__0-515-09007-7	LONGARM AND THE DESPERATE MANHUNT #102	$2.75
__0-515-09056-5	LONGARM AND THE ROCKY MOUNTAIN CHASE #103	$2.75
__0-515-09113-8	LONGARM ON THE OVERLAND TRAIL #104	$2.75
__0-515-09169-3	LONGARM AND THE BIG POSSE #105	$2.75
__0-515-09215-0	LONGARM ON DEADMAN'S TRAIL #106	$2.75
__0-515-09256-8	LONGARM IN THE BIGHORN BASIN #107	$2.75
__0-515-09325-4	LONGARM AND THE BLOOD HARVEST #108 (on sale December '87)	$2.75
__0-515-09378-5	LONGARM AND THE BLOODY TRACKDOWN #109 (on sale January '88)	$2.75
__0-515-09445-5	LONGARM AND THE HANGMAN'S VENGEANCE #110 (on sale February '88)	$2.75

Please send the titles I've checked above. Mail orders to:

BERKLEY PUBLISHING GROUP
390 Murray Hill Pkwy., Dept. B
East Rutherford, NJ 07073

NAME_____

ADDRESS_____

CITY_____

STATE_____ZIP_____

Please allow 6 weeks for delivery.
Prices are subject to change without notice.

POSTAGE & HANDLING:
$1.00 for one book, $.25 for each additional. Do not exceed $3.50.

BOOK TOTAL	$_____
SHIPPING & HANDLING	$_____
APPLICABLE SALES TAX (CA, NJ, NY, PA)	$_____
TOTAL AMOUNT DUE	$_____

PAYABLE IN US FUNDS.
(No cash orders accepted.)

Explore the exciting Old West with one of the men who made it wild!

Please send the titles I've checked above. Mail orders to:

BERKLEY PUBLISHING GROUP
390 Murray Hill Pkwy., Dept. B
East Rutherford, NJ 07073

NAME_____

ADDRESS_____

CITY_____

STATE_____ ZIP_____

Please allow 6 weeks for delivery.
Prices are subject to change without notice.

POSTAGE & HANDLING:
$1.00 for one book, $.25 for each
additional. Do not exceed $3.50.

BOOK TOTAL	$_____
SHIPPING & HANDLING	$_____
APPLICABLE SALES TAX (CA, NJ, NY, PA)	$_____
TOTAL AMOUNT DUE	$_____

PAYABLE IN US FUNDS.
(No cash orders accepted.)

MEET STRINGER MacKAIL
NEWSMAN, GUNMAN, LADIES' MAN

LOU CAMERON'S
STRINGER

"STRINGER's the hardest ridin',
hardest fightin' and hardest lovin' hombre
I've had the pleasure of encountering
in quite a while."
—*Tabor Evans, author of the LONGARM series*

It's the dawn of the twentieth century
and the Old West is drawing to a close. But for
Stringer MacKail, the shooting's just begun.

__0-441-79064-X	**STRINGER**	$2.75
__0-441-79022-4	**STRINGER ON DEAD MAN'S RANGE #2**	$2.75
__0-441-79074-7	**STRINGER ON THE ASSASSINS' TRAIL #3**	$2.75
__0-441-79078-X	**STRINGER AND THE HANGMAN'S RODEO #4** (On sale January '88)	$2.75

Please send the titles I've checked above. Mail orders to:

BERKLEY PUBLISHING GROUP
390 Murray Hill Pkwy., Dept. B
East Rutherford, NJ 07073

NAME_____

ADDRESS_____

CITY_____

STATE_____ZIP_____

Please allow 6 weeks for delivery.
Prices are subject to change without notice.

POSTAGE & HANDLING:
$1.00 for one book, $.25 for each
additional. Do not exceed $3.50.

BOOK TOTAL	$_____
SHIPPING & HANDLING	$_____
APPLICABLE SALES TAX (CA, NJ, NY, PA)	$_____
TOTAL AMOUNT DUE	$_____

PAYABLE IN US FUNDS.
(No cash orders accepted.)